After the Good War

After the Good War

A LOVE STORY

PETER ROGER BREGGIN

STEIN AND DAY/*Publishers*/New York

First published in 1972
Copyright © 1972 by Peter Roger Breggin
Library of Congress Catalog Card No. 72-80344
All rights reserved
Published simultaneously in Canada by Saunders of Toronto, Ltd.
Designed by David Miller
Printed in the United States of America
Stein and Day/*Publishers*/7 East 48 Street, New York, N.Y. 10017
ISBN 0-8128-1492-4

For Phyllis

and

for Mary

After the Good War

1st Entry

This is *the* day of my life, and this entry in the Year 112 After the Good War must become the first in my Journal. All others, days, years and entries, now seem trivial and without feeling.

I spent this day alone on the mountain with the woman, J. A. R. D. Gambol. But instead of Making Her in the Love Bag as I had planned, I found her becoming a part of my most private and treasonous experience. She joined me in the glow that surrounds my Great Book Hallucination.

On my way to see her, National Weather Control was functioning as usual, and I was naked except for my sandals, the transparent Ball Pack around my genitals, and the palm-sized Pleasure Pack stuck firmly to the middle of my chest. I was, of course, appropriately Sealed In with the clear film that Dynamos and Good Lays must spray over their entire bodies. It made my Public Hair glisten in a luxurious triangle rising from within my pop-open Ball Pack and expanding into a great diamond of gray and black curls.

At the Security Monitor in Gambol's corridor I announced myself: "T. E. P. Rogar, O.B., O.B.P., NAMS, Chief Historian for Oldtime 20th Century, to see J. A. R. D. Gambol, Chief Psychologist for Female Wishfulfillment." I was passed without being asked to show my Mental Health Credit Card.

She was waiting for me in her office, working over her Communications Tube, her downy brown hair falling over her naked shoulders. She seemed as careless as ever about appearance—her shoulders hardly glistened with Seal-In—and, as she turned to me, I noticed that the wires of her Pleasure Pack were unstrung.

"Flaunting a disregard for Pleasure?" I asked her.

"I was expecting *you,* Rogar, not an Official," she said, but she did string herself up behind her ears and beneath her transparent Cup.

"We've been Making Up Work for the Government all week, Gambol. We've been at a dozen Committee Meetings. But we never Take any Pleasure together."

She waited, returning no hints.

"Care to Blow Off with me?" I pressed her.

"Where to?"

"Anywhere you want," I said.

"Let's go to the mountains."

"I know just the place."

Gambol did not turn on her Pleasure Pack as we walked down the corridors toward the Bubble Pad. But her great wide eyes signaled some internal preoccupation, which doubtless led the Bureaucrats we passed to assume that she was lost in her favorite Impulse

Pattern. Such self-absorption in a woman made me uneasy, and I tuned in to an Impulse Pattern of my own.

Out on the Pad, we mounted the Conveyor and moved down rows of magnetic Bubbles glistening in the sun. Then we disembarked in front of mine, a transparent two-seater sphere with an adjustable negative charge to carry it through the positive Magnetic Fields. Gambol paused for a moment, pulled a pink ribbon from deep within her hair, and tied it around the ankle of one of the four little ducklike suction feet that hold the Bubble inches above the ground.

It was, of course, against regulations.

She grinned. "Who will look at his *feet?*"

I looked at her sandled feet. They were enormous. And around one ankle she wore another pink ribbon, not much thicker than a thread. That too is against regulations, a sign of narcissism.

We entered through the Portal, breast-stroking to part the Pushthrough Plastic. I topcharged the Bubble, it swooshed rapidly into the air, we were on our way toward the Magnetic EYE in the distance.

Sitting Bubble-close to Gambol I again felt her largeness, the great softness of her flesh, slope upon slope—cheek, neck, and smooth round shoulders—on down her naked body. And the eyes she turned upon me left me blinking back as into a strobe light.

We were uneventfully Swallowed and Spit Out by the EYE, a daily commuter ritual that nonetheless still fills me with apprehension.

[11]

Another Bubble jostled us without touching, our mutually repellent negative charges keeping us at a safe distance. All around us, Bubbles spread out over the land like a giant stream from a child's bubble pipe, a flying shower of spheres fanning out and thinning, scattering into the wind and space.

We passed beyond the monuments and government buildings and over the Stacks of Cubes where the Bureaucrats live, and then past the enormous standing oblongs of The People's Highrises. A Restricted Area loomed ahead, surrounded by a haze, like heat rising from the pavement—an Electronic Screen to strip away the charge from a trespassing Bubble.

Some of these Restricted Areas may be homes where the children of our society are raised in secret. But where the little Cocksuckers come from is purely speculative, and no NOW American can recall CHILD-HOOD.

Dead ahead, the mountains became a backdrop for the United American Rocket Pad, with twenty ships pointing toward the sky. And then the mountains were upon us—green and golden in the sunlight, fresh and tender as if they could be known with a touch.

Rising easily in a warm breeze, we Bubbled over the foothills. Then I gradually discharged us down upon a deserted Pad and led Gambol a short climb through stubby, gnarled evergreens onto the great flat rock from where we could look out over the Blue Ridge Mountains of Virginia and the Shenandoah Valley.

Standing there by myself in the golden light of a

sundown, I have on other occasions felt mystery and awe, the ambiance of my Great Book Hallucination.

Mists filled the valley; the reservoir and heated river evaporated into the atmosphere, bathing the great basin space within the mountains. Across the valley and out into the plain stretched ancient farms, fallow for two centuries, all now converted into Grouper Retreats. Far to the north a single Pollution Stack belched a lovely red pollutant into the atmosphere, surrounding itself in a rich red haze, an artificial sunset. The sun toward the horizon quivered in its own heat, yet the man-made breezes of National Weather Control swept cool air across the valley and the mountains.

Just above the valley floor, Bubbles sailed along, winking beneath the sun as they carried Groupers from one Retreat to another.

Gambol remained motionless except for her strong breathing.

Many times I've taken Professional Playgirls to the mountains and into the Love Bag, but never had I spent so long in silence with a Good Lay. I could hear the sounds of birds, insects, and rustling trees; here in the near-silence, my body vibrated to every sound like a taut drumhead.

A NAMS skywriter rocket drew an Official Message in the sky:

GROUP WORSHIP OF THE GROUP
PREVENTS
THE HEBREW DISEASE

[13]

The Hebrew Disease! As if the message is meant for me. As if they know about my Great Book Hallucination!

Gambol looked up casually at the sky.

"I'm not used to sitting in silence with a Good Lay nearly In the Bag," I told her.

"You think I'm nearly In the Bag?" An ironic twist to the corner of her mouth. A Put-down? Should I feel ashamed?

I was growing melancholy, and again I was surprised to find Gambol undisturbed by my silence. She was staring into the sky—not at the skywriting, but beyond it into something that must be within herself.

"I don't mind the silence, Rogar. Silence isn't painful to me."

"It can't be pleasurable, either."

She smiled in her way again, slightly crooked, perhaps suppressing a chronic grimace over life. She could not have practiced Facial Expressions in Group.

At work the other Dynamos say she has Pleasure Hangups. Bagging her would be a triumph.

But I find myself drawn to her by something different, something dangerous and illicit: her privacy arouses me.

A slight sickness came over me. A touch of the Hebrew Disease? I should be Obliviating myself in a Frantasy with some little Cocksucker. People have needs, and Love Sucks and Fucks. But going off alone damned near privately, that poses a threat to the entire Democratic bureaucracy.

And Gambol? She radiated a presence more power-

[14]

ful than the rising mists and warm odor of the pines and wild grass, more powerful than the message slowly fading in the sky; a presence that made the silence greater.

She was steaming a little from the effort of the climb and the heat of the sun upon the rock, her body seeping right through her scanty film of Seal-In. This woman was not wearing the normal scents to detoxify the human smell, for her odor was as ripe as the very odors of nature, arousing some secret and treasonous sensitivity in me. And no wonder, for the odor seemed to rise from her lap!

Does she use no hygiene on her Public Offering? Is she some sort of raw female?

Now she kicked over a patch of turf, and I caught a whiff of decaying organic matter; damp, rich, and warm.

She pressed the sod back into place with her foot.

The odor is hers! Sweet yet sour, the forbidden odor of woman!

It is said that before Female Hygiene, Oldtime women used to secrete fluids and emit odors when sexually excited. No wonder we now make love only In the Bag!

"You're so intent upon me," she said at last.

I blushed down to the roots of my Public Hair.

"I don't mind your watching me," she said. "It gives me a feeling of your presence."

"You never look at me," I said.

"I look at you more than you realize, Rogar, but you always glance away and blush."

I blushed.

"Besides, Rogar, could we stand it if we turned our eyes upon each other?"

"I can hardly handle your sounds as you sit beside me," I told her, not daring to mention her odor.

"My sounds?"

"The way you breathe so deeply, the way you move so deliberately, the way your voice is so certain and sure, the way you sometimes lick your lips."

We were doing no Songs and Dances, no Angry Displays, no Loving Gestures, none of the stock in trade of Groupers. This woman's quiet face expressed more in its restraint than any Grouper's in an Obliviating Frantasy.

Her eyes, her greatest beauty, were large and splendid and her face was broad, making her look vastly open and yet completely contained. Her eyebrows were deep brown like her eyes, and thickly grown. Her nose was strong, with a high ridge and chiseled nostrils. And her chin, a soft nubbin within the molding of her full cheeks and neck, was too small and indistinct for so much flashing mouth.

It was certain she had never had her face surgically plasterized.

Her hair grew in disorder from a careless mid-part, the ends falling uneven and ragged between her breasts. And her breasts were not full enough for so large a woman. They were broadly set, and her nipples looked as unused as a Cocksucker's. Her breasts gave no stimulus to suckle or to do a Dependent Thing with her.

[16]

Yet the shoulders were soft, strong but inviting, molded so firmly to her long soft arms.

And that belly of rolled flesh: a deep wink was all that hinted of a bellybutton. No clean, tight Playgirl hole to stick my tongue into; Gambol's was a place to explore, a place to unfold and to enter. Could she drive a man to lust without the Bag?

She seemed a child, somewhere between a Cocksucker and a very young Lay; but her strength and softness made her seem in her middle twenties or a little older; perhaps nearly my age.

"You're looking at me hard again," she said. Then, seeing my embarrassment, "No man's look has given me such feelings."

"I get feelings in Group all the time," I told her.

Again that flicker at the corner of her lip. I'd offended her; perhaps no other men desired her. Certainly no Dynamo would say of her, "She's really NOW!" or, "She takes the Pain out of Pleasure!"

How did she ever get to be an Official Beautiful Person?

And what is a Dynamo like me doing with her?

I am told by My Girl that I'm a marvelous specimen from the bottom up. My legs are well formed, and I have a firm ass with a large dimple on each butt and that deep sway of the lower back common to heavy-shouldered athletes. I have so powerful a neck that My Girl can recognize me from a distance in a mob of Groupers. Yet my face, I'm told, is my most interesting

[17]

Public Self. My eyes are deep-set and green, and my salt-and-pepper hair is long and wavy, so that I project a rugged but not unkempt manliness.

But Gambol won't even try to play Sweet Games with me.

I want to dig into her, into those crevices all over her body: that softness between her breast and armpit, another sweet place just under her chin, another where her belly folds upon itself, another in the crease behind her knee, another where her buttocks roll so firmly over and under the back of her thighs.

I raised my hand in a Tender Gesture, but I could not carry out a standard Grouper move with her. Something else was required; my arms and hands became a confused tangle.

Though she sat beside me, she seemed to sit by herself, the way great cats sun themselves together. And Gambol seemed to glow in the sun—to radiate with some of the golden light that fills and pervades my Great Book Hallucination, that most treasonous of all my private experiences.

"You seem to radiate," she told me.

"Gambol, you too. You look tawny in the sun."

I became dizzy, like a young Dynamo with his first Cocksucker. "Gambol," I asked. "Are you in Dependency with anyone?"

"No, I've never had a Dependent."

"Never called anyone 'My Man'?"

"And never will."

[18]

"You sound like a confirmed Nondependent. I don't have an *Official* Dependent, but I do have My Girl. We've sworn to Mutual Emotional Dependency. Someday we'll make it an Official Contract."

"You can do whatever you want, Rogar." And then, more gently, "Do you love her?"

"Of course I do. I'm as Emotionally Dependent as any NOW American male."

Gambol smiled, wetting her lips with her tongue, then recited an Official Truism:

A Man Lives Through His Woman
And a Woman Through Her Man
And They Both Live Through Each Other
And Their Whole Group Lives Through Them.

And then she added, triumphantly, "And Love Fucks in the Bag."

I had never heard anyone mock our NOW Life Principles.

"Rogar," she said. "It's getting dark. Lights are coming on in the valley." She leaned down on her knees and wrapped her arms around herself. Then she confessed another treason: "I have never felt that I belong to NOW."

"I've never been much of a Group Worshiper myself. Do you keep your Grouper Obligations?"

"Only enough to protect my Official Bureaucrat status."

[19]

A great shadow was slowly edging toward us, and looking up, we could see the sun about to disappear behind a peak. Sun, mountain peak, and the sundial shadow pointing toward us seemed to focus all of nature's attention upon our moment together. But I could find no words to share with her.

In a matter of seconds it grew darker and cooler.

I moved close beside her warm soft buttock and thigh, and reached beneath her transparent Cup to rest my hand upon the muff and mound of her Public Offering.

She turned and looked hard at me, but did not push my hand away.

"Gambol, your body—"

"Rogar, I am very, very shy. No one has ever touched me this way."

Negative Feedback? Positive Reinforcement? I was baffled by her signals.

My hand upon her body grew warm, the warmth spreading up my arm, neck, and shoulders.

Her eyes became pools. *Pools!* As if she might break that awesome Grouper Commandment: "Thou Shalt not SPREAD TEARS."

Not being an Official, I've never seen a woman cry. Nor, of course, a man.

"Do you want to give me some Feedback? I *need* Feedback," I said.

"I haven't taken your hand from beneath my cup, Rogar," she said. "What more can I say to you about myself and my feelings?"

I lifted my other hand to her face and touched her.

[20]

Her mouth broke, and I stroked an even smile into her parted lips.

"I could take you for My Girl," I said.

She stiffened so abruptly that I pulled back my hand, popping her Cup.

"I *told* you! I won't be anyone's Girl."

"But why?"

"I am Independent, that's why!"

To think of a woman using such an archaic word—and applying it to herself! And I am growing frightened that I won't want *anyone* to be My Girl after being with Gambol.

She was still glowing, though the night had fallen; and I began to feel as if we were within the same Hallucination.

"I want to kiss you, Gambol."

She parted her lips, and I tasted her.

Uneasy waves of feeling.

She placed her hand upon my heart, beside my Pleasure Pack. Her palm pushed upon me but her fingers felt my skin and my breaths and my heartbeats.

We smiled at each other, and I trembled; so slightly that only the tension in my body told me I must be trembling.

"I have to Withdraw for a while," she said. It was the first Grouper expression I had heard her use, and I waited for her to stand up and do a Release Exercise or an Angry Thing or some other Song and Dance to reassure herself. But she simply sat contained and motionless, absorbing me in those great brown eyes.

Then she placed her hand upon my thigh.

[21]

Snap! The golden glow was gone, like the closing of the Great Book, the way my Vision vanishes before I can read the message.

I sat upright, sure an Official hand waited to seize me for an Attitude Check.

"I'm sorry," Gambol said, and took back her hand.

"No, leave your hand on me, please."

She returned it to my thigh, again palm down; large, soft, firm, warm, a hand upon me in a whole new way. She was not teasing me, not squeezing sensations into my leg and pike. Not hanging on to me, either, nor seeking Dependency. Her hand simply rested with all its weight upon me, all its warmth, the warmth of this whole great person and this whole great day.

She put her life force upon me.

I looked up, expecting to see the sun again.

The evening birds sang, and the insects hummed and sawed, and Gambol's lips parted as we looked through our eyes into our bodies.

She glanced down at where my pike had Popped my Pack. My pike looked back up at us, eye to eye, and released one clear drop of fluid.

A Dynamo should never Pop his Pack, but I was bursting to feel her sweet tongue slide out to take my drop.

She placed both her hands upon me, my balls gently held in so large a hand, and she tenderly stripped a thin stream of clear fluid from within me: like nectar from a honeysuckle.

She drew out my feelings as she drew out my fluid.

[22]

"Even when I was a little Cocksucker, I never did this willingly, never when it was a duty," she whispered as she leaned her face down into my lap. Her hair tumbled over me, hiding her face; and she drank me—a long sweet silent sipping.

I took her head within my hands, the great strong head pressing into my lap. This mighty woman, she seemed to lift me on her shoulders, turning and turning me, drinking me down in a toast to the evening.

She propped me up and lifted her face; Gambol, surfacing like a sleek water animal from my lap's pool.

I began acting without reason, sliding my hand up her leg and into her lap, feeling her curls of Public Hair, parting her flesh with my fingertips.

She wears no cunt liner!

And now she opens to my fingers and I do what no NOW man may do—I reach *inside* her unprotected body.

Her body draws me in and I stir her with my hand, turning my hand slowly within her; and I smell her female odor rising—meaty, rich, heavy—and the smell is good. The smell is good!

Still looking into her eyes, still taking her in and being taken in, I bring my fingers to my mouth; and as she watches, wide-eyed, I smell her and taste her and suck my fingers clean.

She is sitting so strong and impassive—so marvelously within herself and within her own feelings—that I hardly realize what is happening. Her lips, her face, then her body begin trembling.

I am just in time to catch her as she totters over.

[23]

2nd Entry

REMEMBER THE GOOD WAR

In celebration of the year 2100 We the People of the United States launched our all-out Preventive War against the rest of mankind, and, despite the gloom-doom predictions of centuries past, we won the War hands down with hardly a casualty. All our enemies were either annihilated or rendered harmless, and for the first time in history, our nation reigned and still reigns with absolute sovereignty over the entire earth.

In recognition of the end of Oldtime and the beginning of NOW TIME, or simply NOW, the calendar was begun anew, and the year of our victory, 2100, became the Year 1 A.G.W., After the Good War.

Each NOW American—Dynamo or Good Lay, even the little Cocksuckers who pass through the great electronic archway at NAMS—must Imprint these words.

I no longer accept NOW History.

I, the Chief NAMS Historian for the Twentieth Century, in secret write my own history about the events After the Good War.

[25]

Should I be found out, either for my Journal, or for my private thoughts, or for my illicit feelings for J. A. R. D. Gambol, I would be stripped of all status. But worse, my treason might cause NAMS to commit me to a Pleasure Hospital. There the Psychiatric Officials could Cap me for Remote Control or force me to stimulate my Pleasure Center in endless preoccupation.

Or, with more finality, they might plant the Pleasure Probe within my brain. Yet I must pursue my Great Book Hallucination and my research into the Hebrew Disease.

My last Hallucination came upon me two weeks ago. My eyes were weary from researching Oldtime materials on the printed page, and I began to drowse off; falling into a slow growing light, then opening my eyes into a richer luster, like antique gold glimmering in firelight. I cannot imagine its source, but it is the same golden light that bathes me and Gambol when we are alone together.

I loll within this light—eyes open, hypnotized by it, and yet awake and alert, my breathing as through great musical tubes, my fingers tender to every texture beneath them; and I feel that great weight upon me, the ancient open book upon my chest, the large letters and the message, and as the message materializes before my eyes, just at the moment of recognition the book vaporizes amid a showering burst of gold. Then the glow fades away.

I do not know for whom I write my Journal, or if I shall be read, but I write with a greater purpose than personal release. My Vision sustains me and draws me on. I must communicate all I know about NOW, even the details of our lives. And so, today:

Another typical Washington, D.C., day, as the Conveyor Belt carried me from the Bubble Pad across the campus of NAMS: uninterrupted warm, dry sunshine mixed with a rainbow sprinkle at the hour appointed and announced beforehand by National Weather Control. It was pure pleasure to be Conveyed naked beneath the sun, body-close to a thousand Good Lays and Dynamos on their way across the nation's greatest bureaucracy—NAMS, the National Agency for Mental Security.

But while the weather was in hand over most of the nation this morning, there were reports of an Emotional Squall in New England, a slight tendency toward Depression in the Middle West, and some Schizoid Loss of Interest in the Public Good in California. Ironic that we can control the weather but not the nation's mood.

Each morning I learn from my home Q Tube what kind of day it will be for me. As the President speaks to the nation, each citizen sits before the Q Tube with his fingers on his Touch Tone Mood Meter, responding to each word the President offers, while behind the President the Gallop Billboard blinks and bleeps the nation's responses to him. This is called Galloping Feedback, though the derivation of "gallop" is uncertain; perhaps it comes from the practice of flashing the winners on a big board at Oldtime horse races. Hence the NOW expression, "A nation gallops on its feedback."

If something the President has said offends or upsets or depresses too many citizens, he can explain it away on the spot, or, if need be, reverse himself immediately in the interest of Public Mental Health.

Such a responsive political system makes each day an uncertainty for me, for if the Galloping Feedback becomes critical, I will be mobilized as all of NAMS goes to work Making Up Wishfulfillments to offer the nation on the President's next Daily Hour.

What did I Touch-tone into my Mood Meter this morning? I lied. I gave typical Grouper responses. What else could I have done? Signaled that I, a Bureaucrat, might have the Hebrew Disease? Panic throughout the city!

It's said that every Bureaucrat's Mood Meter is Buggered by a direct tap into NAMS, and that the Chief Bugger's Office is the nation's most powerful. Hence the expression "I've been Buggered" expresses each man's most personal vulnerability to government intervention. But most Bureaucrats accept Buggering as a natural part of our lives, for our mental health affects the mental health of the nation. Yes, every Bureaucrat lives in Mutual Emotional Dependency with his countrymen. This is the meaning of the NAMS slogan, "We who *own* the people *owe* the people."

Now the Conveyor Belt slides me by a Morale Booster flashing an Official Truism:

LOVE FUCKS

in

THE BAG

[28]

I have not fucked Gambol in the Bag. Once or twice each week we have Blown Off in my Bubble to sit together talking and touching upon the great rock that overlooks the valley. How we touch! Sometimes I will kiss her and fondle her, feeling her breasts swelling in my hands, feeling her nipples come alert, feeling her whole body alive to me. She who did not know she could have sensations in her breasts! But still she will not go into the Bag with me.

Doesn't every woman yearn to be Bagged?

The Conveyor moves like one enormous flat snake, slithering along as far as the eye can see with a thousand people upon its back. Now it is moving within the Campus Playground of NAMS, where the plastic grass undulates in waves of blue, green, and gold.

It is difficult to visualize, but we are told that before the great Antipollution Mobilization of the year 2036, only sixty-four years Before the Good War, Washington, D.C., was once black and blue and gray with soot and other debris. Although our national industrial cartel, United American Goodwill Industries, Inc., had warned us that it was dangerous to tamper with the ecological balance produced by man's natural waste products, we nonetheless began to clear the air of the substances that had turned our nation into a dark death mask of itself.

Industry's propollution warnings turned out to be well founded. When man's waste products were at last reduced to pre-twentieth-century levels, the balance between man and nature was so upset that the molds, long suppressed by pollution, began to proliferate,

[29]

covering the land with green and yellow slime. Civilization began to mildew! The rest of our vegetation began to die, and everything made of wood rotted. And while the Pollution Stacks were being built to repollute the atmosphere with the natural inhibitors of the Great Mold, NAMS constructed this artificial Campus Playground, now a unique monument to the time when we were mildewing from an overzealous and unnatural effort to clean up our environment.

Here at NAMS, both the nation's mood and its pollution are monitored and kept at sufficiently high levels. And as the Sky Clock comes into view, I recall rumors that even the passage of time is regulated, according to the time the President requires to fulfill his daily promises.

The Conveyor is carrying me directly beneath the Sky Clock, a floating sphere as large as the largest building, a giant, negatively charged immobile Bubble held in suspension by intersecting positive magnetic fields. On its side are the words THE TIME IS NOW. No more Oldtime segmentation—one time in Washington, D.C., another in California, another in some Conquered Land. NOW Time, originating here in Washington, is the One Correct Time for the world.

I'm too early for my meeting with Gambol. In my anxiety, I have hurried where I am afraid to go.

I take another Conveyor past the National Center for SIMPLIFICATIONS, the hub of political and behavioral science research, and the source of the great

SIMPLIFICATIONS so important in the President's Daily Hour. Its Electronic Screen is blinking out a new one:

PEOPLE NEED MACHINES
and
MACHINES NEED PEOPLE

Standing nearby is the monument revered as our truest cathedral to the past: a slender, tall missile hull painted Day-glo orange with two great Day-glo balls nestled at the shaft's base. It is called America's Most Proud Erection, and bears the motto: "For a hundred years these proud erections responded to our deepest needs for security."

Then follows the explanation that begins, "Nearly overcome by the Green Mold and surrounded by the Red Tide, we nonetheless . . ."

Eventually we did suppress the Green Mildew, but the Red Tide proved a more difficult adversary. I'm told the Pacific has slowly faded to a pink glow; but from what I've seen, the Atlantic Ocean is as bloody red as ever, as are the beaches and even the towns and cities along the shore. The villain is a harmless but prodigious biologic dye, a red microorganism known from Biblical Times that first proliferated in earnest sometime after the land began to mildew. The Red Tide was, of course, blamed on the Chinese Communist Conspiracy—an attempt to engulf us in humiliation in the eyes of all the

[31]

world. The alleged release of these microorganisms by the Chinese was used as one more justification for the Good War.

Was the Green Slime also a grim Chinese joke? America overcome by a Red Tide and rotted away by a Dollar Green Mildew? Despite Official History, I have come to believe that the Red Tide, as much as the Green Mildew, was the result of our frantic last-ditch Antipollution campaign. The rivers, long polluted, responded to the cleanup with this infestation, which spread into the salt water, where it thrived, and still thrives. It has proven too difficult to repollute the rivers and the seacoast without the all-out industrial commitment to pollution of the Twentieth Century. Pollution no longer pays.

The Electronic Screen beside the monument is playing an interesting segment of Official History:

In 1990, 110 years B.G.W., with the world apparently on the verge of atomic war, citizens of all the atomic powers began to flee from the population centers and from the missile sites. As the world moved inexorably still nearer to conflict, panic-stricken citizens began an exodus from these nations, seeking refuge in their satellites and territories. In America orders were issued to seal off the borders against escape, and NAMS boldly declared, "The People must not abandon their Missiles and their Military."

Once the people were successfully returned to their Military and their Missiles, grateful military leaders declared a National Celebration, called the Great Roundup; and "RALLY 'ROUND THE MISSILE!" resounded throughout the nation as the inspiration for

[32]

our first massive Group Worships. Hence to this day the President has an Erection on his front lawn each NOW New Year—a giant Day-glo missile, the tallest in the land, to celebrate our new religion, Group Worship of the Group.

I Imprint all this in a matter of seconds, using the technique which allows any normal citizen to absorb the Truth at 2500 words per minute with perfect understanding, complete acceptance, and excellent recall on Citizenship Tests.

Lately I sometimes find myself reading more slowly, almost ponderously by NOW standards.

As the Sky Clock let out a mellow boom and expelled a red, white, and blue puff of pollutant, signaling the hour, I got up and made my way to the Conveyor leading toward the division of Female Psychology, where Gambol would be helping scan the Women's National Mood.

She was at her Q Tube, twirling the dials and making notes. I stood for a moment watching her.

How different she looks now! Her eyes are less saddened, less heavy in the lids, and her breasts are full where once they sat like mounds upon her chest. Even her Public Hair is more luxurious.

This woman is lovely without Seal-in!

I've begun to neglect my Seal-in, too. My odor makes me think of her!

I've also begun to notice that my Public Hair is thicker, and that my pike has become longer and fuller.

All this without my Bagging her.

[33]

"Hello, Rogar, how are your feelings today?" she asked rather formally.

"My feelings are pure," I responded, and then we both grinned.

"My feelings are full," she said.

"I've never heard that expression in Group."

"You make me full with feelings every time I see you, Rogar."

"Your breasts are ripening," I teased her.

She blushed more than I expected: no Good Lay would blush over a simple compliment.

She turned off her Tube. "Don't we have to Convey over to the library?"

"Yes," I said loudly, for the benefit of any eavesdroppers, "I have some work I should Make Up over there."

Her stride was long, firm, and broad-based like an ice skater's. Her thighs moved more easily than they used to; they seemed trimmer yet even stronger from walking and playing with me.

We walked to the Conveyor that slants off toward the old National Library of Medicine, now the National Information Center for Mental Health and Mental Security (NICMHMS), the national data bank that rates each citizen for Sound Mind and Sound Credit. Each of us carries our Mental Health Credit Card in a slot beneath our Pleasure Pack.

No one was within earshot.

"Rogar, I was gathering information for a SIMPLI-FICATION on Female Sexuality, and I found something that bears on the Hebrew Disease. It's a collection of letters written shortly After the Good War. A fragment of uncatalogued microfilm."

Could she know about my Journal?

"I have it inside my Pleasure Pack, Rogar."

"But how could you fit anything in there?"

She didn't answer.

"You guessed my interest in unofficial history?"

"Rogar, I listen when you talk. Do you still think I'm a Playgirl?"

"HALT!" a voice shouted.

An Attitude Check!

"DISEMBARK!"

We stepped off the Conveyor.

"FREE-ASSOCIATE!"

I went into Free-Association Posture and began to babble, staring all the while into space, my ears alert for Gambol's words, and hoping the Official would not check her Pleasure Pack. They would take her in for a complete Moral Evaluation and Interrogation, probably with drugs.

"Pleasure, pleasure," Gambol was muttering, "so little time for pleasure . . . damn work . . . got to check out this SIMPLIFICATION . . . pleasure, pleasure, I need some pleasure . . . Love Fucks . . . In the Bag . . . Bag that Dynamo, Rogar . . . Rogar in the Bag . . . Oh . . . Oh . . ."

"All right, what was so interesting between the two of you that you didn't even see me coming?"

"I am J. A. R. D. Gambol, O.B., NAMS, Chief

Psychologist for Female Wishfulfillment. There's an Emotional Squall among New England women, and I'm assigned to work up Female Wishfulfillment for the President's Daily Report."

The Official turned to me.

"T.E.P. Rogar, O.B., O.B.P., NAMS, Chief Historian for Oldtime, detailed to Make Up Work with Gambol. We are pressed for time," I lied.

"All right, FREE-ASSOCIATE."

Our streams of consciousness came out smoothly, without inhibitions or other signs of the Hebrew Disease, and the Official told us we could reembark for the library.

He gave Gambol a pinch on her bottom as we stepped back onto the Conveyor.

"You must be looking different." I grinned at her. "Never seen anyone pinch your ass before."

"I don't like it!"

"But you popped out with a wish to go Into the Bag with me."

"I like to throw in Standard Sex for effect when I'm Free-associating," she said curtly.

"Well, at least we're both O.B.P.'s," I said. "We have that in common. Yet you even want to deny that. You left it off your title during the Attitude Check." And then, more solicitously, "You should be careful, Gambol. The Officials pick up those kind of slips."

"I'm not an Official Beautiful Person, Rogar. Can't you tell by looking at me? I'm twenty pounds over the Norm. Not much to Bag."

[36]

I became uncomfortable. "Gambol, how did a Non-O.B.P. get to be so high an Official Bureaucrat?"

"I always came out above the Ninety-fifth percentile on Personality Tests. I have an Outstanding Personality."

A quality Lay in some respects at least, I thought—and then caught myself.

"The Personality Tests are as phony as that Free Association, Rogar. I learned to fake them at a very early age. No one ever knows what I am feeling—no one except you. You already know a little."

"But since CHILDHOOD?" I used the forbidden word. "You've been faking tests all your life?"

She sounded like the Oldtime Independent, declared virtually extinct by that unofficial psychiatrist from the twentieth Century, O. Peter Braggard, M.D., who believed that hardly anyone deserved to be called free and independent anymore. Instead he defined the typical American as a *Non*dependent whose apparent freedom was really an inability to relate to anyone.

My deepest sympathies reach out across the centuries to that Old Braggard, who would have appreciated a woman like Gambol.

The two of us reached NICMHMS.

"Don't you want the microfilm?" Gambol asked me as we separated at the entrance.

I had forgotten. How easily I become caught up with myself in the presence of this woman.

"I'd like to have it," I told her, "if you think it's safe to give it to me here."

[37]

She turned to hide her maneuvers, unsnapped her Pleasure Pack, then closed it again and handed me a small capsule.

I taped it beneath my Pack, using the adhesive I keep there for collecting secret materials.

We were now coupled in Treason, if in nothing more . . .

3rd Entry

All night, images of Obliviating Frantasies flooded my
mind as I lay beside My Girl in our Cube. I saw My Girl
discovering my secret love for Gambol and reporting us
to the Officials. I saw them finding Gambol and me as
we touch each other upon the rock, and I saw them
tearing us apart and dragging us off to the Pleasure
Hospital to Die at Our Machines.

We have learned to install the Pleasure Probe within
the brain of a man so that he will give up all other
activity to stimulate himself into an Obliviating Frantasy; but the pleasure center cannot be separated from
the pain center, and the addicted man will drive himself
on until death. Hence it is said of a man who Takes too
much Pleasure: he will Die at his Machine.

We do not understand the cause of death. Is it too
much pain, or too much pleasure, or the conflict
between the two? Our ignorance covers the entire
matter with as much superstition as the paradoxes of
ancient religion and theology.

Every NOW American must daily face these contra-

[39]

dictions on a smaller scale with his Pleasure Pack. While he cannot plug his Pleasure Pack into his brain, the neuronal terminals do connect directly with the nerves of his genitals and his ears, so that he bombards himself with sensations without the distortions of natural hearing or the vagaries of another person's hands upon his pike and balls. The result is that most men in NOW America live with a low-grade testicular ache from Taking too much Pleasure.

This condition must have a hundred names, depending on your social class. I've heard it called Pleasure Pack Paralysis (PPP) among the Elite and Black Balls among the People. We bureaucrats call it Adam's Ache. How to treat the Ache, how to get the most pleasure for the least pain, is without question the most frequent subject of bantering and serious conversation among Dynamos, whose highest praise for a Good Lay is, "She takes the Pain out of Pleasure." And yet the contrasting expression, "Oh, what a pain," also indicates a woman of overwhelming sensuality. All of which indicates that the average NOW American hasn't made up his mind if a Good Lay eases or exacerbates his Ache.

Whether women also suffer from this paradoxical ache seems to be an unexplored subject among Dynamos.

After lying awake all night, I decided to use my Bureaucrat status to gain a tour of the Pleasure Hospital—something I had put off for years.

In the morning light, my imagination exploded in anticipation of what I'd see: faces contorted in orgiastic pleasure, frenetic motion, extreme Frantasy and total Obliviation, followed by death.

I reassured myself that it would be the best orgasm of a man's life.

At least that: a good last orgasm.

My Secretary arranged a tour for me in the afternoon.

The Tour Guide informed us that no one is shown in the act of Dying at His Machine; medical ethics allows no intrusion upon the best orgasm of a person's life.

This, the only concession to privacy I'd ever heard in NOW America, was accepted by the Groupers in the tour as they accept everything else.

One of them was even Capped—probably under Remote Control. Nothing seems more lowly to me than a Capped Bureaucrat. They are, of course, ideal for their jobs—docile, single-minded, and lacking in all spontaneity.

We were told that the terminal Obliviating Frantasy takes place in the Last Room, a name that sent unaccountable shivers up and down my spine, even to the tips of my toes. A frightening sensation of something from my CHILDHOOD?

Tuning back into the tour guide, I heard a brief, familiar history of psychosurgery, with special attention to the bravery of a band of several hundred Twentieth Century psychosurgeons who managed to turn back the terrible onslaught of that unofficial psychiatrist, O. Peter Braggard, who, along with a small coterie of

[41]

Unofficial Types, had tried desperately to strangle the progress of mental health technology. But psycho-surgery at last triumphed and gave America what she most sought, domestic tranquility.

Now that the technologies of pleasure preoccupy us, the more extreme measures of the Twentieth Century are rarely employed. Nothing like the mutilation of 50,000 lobotomy patients has been contemplated in recent centuries. In the vast majority of cases, we are told, people now submit willingly, even gratefully, to a technology that offers peace of mind. Most of our older citizens pass quietly away under experimental Caps, while some of the more daring beg to be allowed to go out in Obliviating Frantasy beneath the tongs of the Pleasure Probe.

It was all over by the time we entered the Last Room. We found nothing more than a row of men and women with their Probes implanted, each left unat-tended, each slumped over his or her Machine, puppets strung with wires from the head, each Dead at His Machine.

The guide reassured me that no one witnessing the last hours could doubt the transcendence of their ecstasy over their agony.

"Is it like a *real* orgasm?" I asked, but of course he did not understand what I was talking about. Neither did I.

What would it be like to put my own biologic Probe, my own pike into Gambol's body? A catastrophic

[42]

Frantasy of Pain and Pleasure—Gambol drilled to death,
myself drained and dying upon her body?

I have been Taking very little Pleasure lately, sharing
little or nothing of myself with anyone, skipping Group,
avoiding My Girl, going Into the Bag with no one.
Instead I have been reading the secret capsules Gambol
and I have found, and I have been searching through the
archives, finding pieces of literature that bear upon the
Hebrew Disease. Fragments of the Hebrew Bible keep
turning up, too ineradicably a part of the past for the
Censors to have destroyed totally. I have been reading
and rereading the Old Bible—especially the first five
books, which I have nearly pieced together.

Several passages do seem extraordinarily un-
American. In one, a man named Abraham is told by the
Jewish God that God Himself will destroy a city called
Sodom because of its wickedness. Abraham confronts
this God, asking if He will not spare the city if there are
fifty righteous men within it. God agrees and then
Abraham, apologizing to his Maker—"I who am but dust
and ashes"—demands to know whether God will still
destroy the city if forty-five righteous men are to be
found within it. The bargaining continues until God
concedes that for the safety of ten righteous men He
will spare Sodom. And ultimately God preserves the
smaller city of Zoar to save the family of *one single man*
named Lot.

I believe the expression used to describe tough

[43]

bargaining—"Jew him down"—must have come from this mighty bargaining session. But what does it mean in a religion when a *single man,* "I who am but dust and ashes," can confront God and convince Him on an issue of right and wrong? And when God extends Himself and saves an entire city for the sake of *one righteous man,* what does *that* mean?

I can tell even from my fragments that the Bible is a grossly confused document with many conflicting moral messages, perhaps from widely spaced eras. But consider the importance of this extraordinary INDIVIDUALISM at *any* given moment in man's history.

I also keep coming across fragments of the American Constitution and the Declaration of Independence, documents once so popular that their expurgation also remains incomplete 112 Years After the Good War. These documents, too, seem fraught with contradictions, for they speak of equality and yet make provisions for slavery. At least we are NOW humane enough to provide decent quarters free of labor for the blacks within the confines of the Zoo. But one statement from the Declaration keeps reverberating through my mind:

We hold these truths to be self-evident, that all men are created equal, that they are endowed by their Creator with certain unalienable Rights, that among these are Life, Liberty, and the pursuit of Happiness.

About the only similarity between this and anything I've seen in NOW America is the clever use of capital letters!

But what of this "Life, Liberty, and the pursuit of Happiness"? Whose Happiness? *Everyone* NOW favors the Group's Life, Liberty, and Happiness. Happiness is True Mental Health, and everyone accepts that Mental Health and Well-being is the highest goal, toward which we strive with all our life and liberty.

Where does the Hebrew Disease fit in?

Can IT be caught by reading these documents? Does the Disease touch me in my Great Book Hallucination? Does it somehow bridge the gap between the Old Bible and America's Revolutionary Documents?

There is another fragment from the Old Bible which strikes me as blatantly revolutionary. It is the story of a man named Job. Despite all the worst an arbitrary Jewish God can inflict upon him, Job remains His obedient servant. This might sound like a Grouper story of submissive devotion to ideals higher than oneself; but there is something else about the story: Job endures the most enormous pain and agony, and he does it *entirely by himself.* He defies the Grouper Commandment: "Thou shalt not endure pain alone." A man who can face pain alone threatens our NOW America!

Sometimes I feel like a Hebrew. But being a Hebrew seems so lonely, so heavy a journey through life.

So much reading and thinking left me exhausted, but gratified, and I lay back in my contour recliner beside my Q Tube. I found my eyes closing involuntarily; myself hypnotizing me as my lids closed the last slats between me and the light. The darkness burst back

[45]

into light within my head, and I reclined in a great golden bath, more golden than the most brilliant sun, than all the psychedelic lights going off at orgasm in a Pleasure Dome with a Playgirl; brighter I am sure than the atomic blasts in the Good War that incinerated everyone who Saw the Light.

Sunset gold burning up a lake, sun blazing within a storm of sand, the gold that permeates Oldtime religious painting—these are approximations of the light that bathes me in my Great Book Hallucination.

Lying upon my recliner like a rocket passenger taking off, I became weighted beneath the Great Book, an enormous volume from Oldtime such as I have seen in museums, a book heavy as stone tablets, with leather covers and thick crinkly pages, and I was turning the pages very deliberately, not Imprinting but reading slowly, and the words were powerful, the most powerful I had ever read. The breath in my lungs moving in and out as through great church organ pipes, my heart beating like an Oldtime cathedral bell, and I was reading the most profound meanings of my life.

And then, as always, just when the Great Book's meanings were touching me, exactly at the peak before understanding, my Vision began to fade—the glow weakening, the stone-heavy book growing light, the words fading. And I came out of my Hallucination without remembering one single word in the Great Book.

This time I would not let it escape me!

I called upon my Vision to return. And with shivers

that were neither pain nor pleasure, I lay back, closed my eyes, and reopened myself.

The room began to glow again, and the book was nearly open for my reading when a thought came to me, resounding through my head like spoken words. I heard a Voice—I HEARD A VOICE!

The Voice blasted me out of my Vision, and I came to in a storm of anxiety, excitement, anticipation—

I could not recall what I'd heard.

I lay in my recliner feeling at once like a plaything of Other Forces and like a man of great importance, two roles no longer incompatible.

I must become passive before what is happening within me, before I can become strong with who I am.

Who I am?

The spoken words said something about WHO I AM!

4th Entry

Bible stories of great Jews, Revolutionary Documents—
and NOW Americans dead like sacks of sand at their
Machines!

Again I tossed and turned beside My Girl, and when
I finally did drowse off I awoke in fright from a
nightmare that I could not recall.

Overcome with need for Gambol, I risked Q-tubing
her at her Cube.

"I woke you up?"

"Yes," she mumbled.

"I have to see you this morning. At the usual
place?"

Gambol answered "Yes" without questioning me.

I patted My sleeping Girl, who hardly budged, and
told her I had urgent business at work.

Bubbling toward NAMS to meet Gambol near
America's Most Proud Erection, I watched the approach
of the Needle Eye with apprehension.

Seen from a rocket far above the city, the mile-high
Needles bristle like pins from a relief map. Seen from

my Bubble as I sail at great speed toward one of the Eyes, the Needle ahead looms like a monstrous magic wand poised to smash me from the sky.

This Needle is the largest in the area, six thousand feet tall. It is made up of a dozen separate needles stacked tail to top, one above the other. Each segment is five hundred feet high from its narrow pin base to its wide Eye above. These tall multiwaisted, multi-eyed creatures stare in every direction across the city and the countryside; each a Totem Pole to American Technology.

Around me, early-morning commuters in their negatively charged Bubbles are homing toward the Needles like bees toward a hive, each drawn by the positive charge radiating from the Eye.

We commuters say that the morning's first Passage through the Eye determines luck for the rest of the day.

I'm sucked into the Eye, through the Tube with a gentle, sensual bobbing, and then spit out 1500 feet above the ground as the tunnel's negative charge repels my negative Bubble.

When Bubbling was first proposed, opponents of technology claimed that Americans would refuse to submit themselves daily to an experience that surpasses the most harrowing Oldtime carnival ride. But they were wrong. Ever since the subway and the freeway, not to mention the shuttle jet and helicopter, commuters have responded with nonchalance to hazards that would leave a normal person shaking.

We still do have occasional crashes, of course.

Bubblers have found themselves stalled in the Tube, with another Bubble bearing down upon them. But I've witnessed only one bad accident—about a year ago, I saw a Bubble exit from its Tube to plummet 3000 feet like a stone dropped from a tower. The sun was sparkling on the clear sphere, and I watched every frantic movement of the two occupants until the moment of impact upon the ground.

I do not know how Oldtime commuters stood it—passing by crushed vehicles with injured and dying fellow commuters lying all about and being carried off in screaming ambulances.

Nothing says more about progress in America than our awe of these Needles. Made of pure Theron, the most powerful and lightweight of alloys, these slender supple creatures with their silver heads and steady blue Eyes are sometimes called Therons. Hence the expression "A man of Theron" carries the old sense of a "man of steel," with added connotations of grace, dignity, and aristocratic aloofness. Sometimes the elite speak of themselves as Therons.

As strong as they are, the Therons would bend or topple, especially in a stiff wind caused by a Weather Control failure. But they are supported by their mutual magnetism, each Theron repelling and attracting its neighbors in a complex supportive network. Only a regional electrical power failure could bring all the Bubbles smashing to the earth and all the Theron needles crashing down upon the population. But as every NOW American has been taught, there has never

[51]

been a regional power failure in the entire history of the United States. Still, "a man of Theron" carries uneasy connotations of strength too dependent upon a potentially unsteady system or elite establishment. That is why those citizens who live within the six-thousand-foot radius of a giant Needle have an expression, "Living in the Shadow of the Eye," which speaks both of their faith in modern technology and their dread of its failure.

When I disembarked from the Conveyor in Fountain Park near America's Most Proud Erection on the NAMS campus, Gambol was waiting for me.

I smiled awkwardly, not able to say why I needed to see her. She didn't seem to require an explanation, and we sat beneath artificial trees.

I began explaining my latest Vision in great detail, and she listened without comment.

"You don't think my Vision is insane, Gambol?"

"I don't know what 'insane' means," she said.

She sounded like that Old Braggard who denigrated everything that smacked of psychiatric labeling.

"Crazy. Treasonous. Like my interest in Revolutionary Jews."

"Crazy?" She thought it over. "Sometimes I think I am crazy."

"Oh, go shame a Jew!"

"I don't know what *that* means, either," she said angrily.

[52]

She knew very well that this expression refers to the utter futility of trying to embarrass oldtime Jews.

"And sometimes," I said, "I don't know if your clever cynicism reflects a true intelligence."

I got up, and she lagged behind me as we walked around the outskirts of the trees.

I saw an Official, off to our left, coming toward us!

"Gambol," I whispered. "He's seen us Taking Each Other Too Seriously."

We both adjusted our Pleasure Packs and began tapping our ear and genital terminals as if preoccupied with Pleasure. Still the Official kept approaching. We hurried to catch up to the early commuters moving toward a Conveyor.

"Attitude Check! Attitude Check!"

The Group around us became a babbling flock of Dynamos, Good Lays, and Cocksuckers; each face blank, each tongue loosened in a stream of Unself-consciousness.

I could see the Official, a rather old one, eyeing a young man from top to bottom, studying his Stream for signs of the Hebrew Disease.

At least he isn't after us!

But I am too labile today—too responsive, not sufficiently exhausted with Pleasure. If the Official stops in front of me he'll see the feelings pulsing through my skin, the telltale blush in the center of my chest, the nervous flexion of my thighs. I do flex them too much in public.

Our nakedness makes us so defenseless, forces us to withdraw *further* into ourselves and thus buries us within our own skin as surely as if our skin were a suit of plastic and rubber.

Plastic and rubber? I'm sweating right through my Seal-in, a single stream down my armpit. No—I forgot to Seal Myself In this morning! If he stops in front of me and gives me a Palm Test, I'll be "sweating like a Jew."

I kept on with my Associations: "Suck, fuck, pump the Bag, squeeze, breeze, and blow me good, I'm a Dynamo for sure, working, loving, playing, fucking. Oh, it's good to feel so free . . ."

When the Official finally got back on the Conveyor, Gambol and I sat down again beneath some plastic trees.

Wanting so much to touch her, I was afraid the first tender feeling would Pop My Pack.

"That was close," she murmured.

"You had trouble Free-Associating? So did I!"

"I kept thinking about your attack on my 'clever cynicism.' Is that what you think of me?"

"No, I just keep falling back into Grouper talk with you even when I don't like it. I tell you to 'go shame a Jew' the very next day after reading about great Jews. And when you refuse to Fake It with me, I get angry."

"You are learning so much," she said.

I blushed for all the world to see, and again I regretted my nakedness. I want to blush for her, not for NOW America.

A young couple passed by us, arguing as they walked. He was tired; she wanted to Take Pleasure with him at a Pleasure Dome. Exasperated, she gave him a Grouper order:

"Do Your Thing!"

Instantly his face contorted in rage. He danced around her, shaking his fists, stamping his feet, taking mock punches at her—a fine Temper Tantrum. In a minute or two he was out of breath.

"Feel better?" she asked him.

He nodded and then gave her the command:

"Do *Your* Thing!"

She came very close to him and eyed him ceremoniously; then she began moving her hands all over his skin, barely touching him, a sculptor putting finishing touches on wet clay, modeling his face and his shoulders and his chest, and, now, down on her knees smoothing his thighs and his legs.

"Into the Bag," they agreed, and, fully reconciled, skipped off toward a Pleasure Dome.

"Should I do My Thing?" I asked Gambol.

She grimaced.

Gambol makes me so defensive. She can be so *certain* about herself.

Oh, for a young Cocksucker!

I feel an uneasy crawling sensation between my legs.

Should I confess to Gambol that I seldom fuck anyone except My Girl? Tell her the worst—that my body had felt dead for years, until I met her?

She makes me realize how uncritically this historian accepts NOW America. Gambol sees with her own eyes!

How did she get that way?

No one today has any sense of his personal history, not with CHILDHOOD blanked out, and I don't dare stir that up, even within so strong a woman.

I am afraid to go THERE myself. Not alone, and I cannot ask her to do it with me.

I need help. But where to seek it in NOW America? Autonomie Institute?

"Are you angry when I talk about Bagging you?" I asked Gambol.

She looked down, a great shy girl, her hair falling over her face, her shoulders hunched like those of a big soft boy who'd been given a licking. I want to lift her chin, but that would mean encountering those eyes.

"Answer me, will you? Are you upset at me?"

"You sound upset about yourself, Rogar."

"I feel fine."

"Fine?"

I may be suffering from a fatal case of the Hebrew Disease.

"I tell you so much, Gambol, even about my Visions, and then I feel judged by your silence. I *care* what you think."

She shook her head. "No one has ever cared."

"Where have you been all your life? In a shell?"

"Yes, Rogar."

"I'm sorry. I didn't mean to make fun of you."

"My feelings aren't hurt, Rogar, I was agreeing with you. I've been in a shell all my life, so I don't think anything inside you could sound strange to me."

"I have nightmares, too." I confessed another sign of Disease. "That's why I called you this morning."

[56]

"What kind?"

I became frightened, as I said, "Sometimes there are others in my dreams, maybe even little children."

"Cocksuckers, you mean?"

"No, Gambol, *very little* children come into my dreams."

"Please don't talk to me about that." It was the only time she'd ever Shut me Off.

I felt the Dread of CHILDHOOD. "Out of sight, out of mind" is the only aphorism about little children in NOW America.

I still could not recall this morning's nightmare.

We walked on for a while, and then Gambol turned to me and said, "I dream little tiny children are being beaten."

We walked on again, my own thoughts turned toward Taking Pills.

"Do you think it's possible we were beaten long ago, Rogar?"

I shrugged and thought of the Cocksuckers, who can sometimes be heard singing to themselves:

> YOUR CHILDHOOD IS GONE
> YOUR CHILDHOOD IS DEAD
> RING AROUND A ROSIE
> PUT YOURSELF TO BED

"Sometimes, Rogar, I think I'm so large because I'm trying to hide a little CHILD deep within me. Not just hiding it—protecting it, keeping it out of *their* sight. It's almost like I'm pregnant."

We both glanced around apprehensively.

Women never speak of getting pregnant. Women never *get* pregnant! Sometimes a woman disappears and never reappears again, and it's suspected that she became pregnant making love Outside the Bag. Sometimes she will reappear months later, this time a Capped Woman whose feelings will never get out of control.

Many men prefer Capped Women nowadays.

"I owe myself to my largeness," she went on. "I'm sure it's kept me from ruining myself as some man's Dependent or as a Playgirl."

Her soft brown eyes were downcast, her hair unkempt, and she walked with that awkward swagger so unlike a Good Lay.

"Rogar, have you ever thought about the little black children in the Zoo?"

"I was thinking about them this morning, before I called you."

"For all we know," she said, "the black women in the Zoo are the only ones who can get pregnant and have children."

"What are you getting at?"

"Maybe we were all black children to begin with, Rogar. Maybe they bleach those of us who are sent out to join NOW America as Cocksuckers. The others could be kept behind to become colored adults to raise more children in the Zoo."

"And the bleaching process sterilizes us? Most whites do look sterile and washed out compared to the blacks we see."

[58]

But we could not have been raised in the Zoo. No matter how well they cleaned out our memories, we'd be bound to recognize HOME when we saw it again.

That idea stirred me—seeing HOME again.

Perhaps I will never understand myself and NOW America until I find out where the CHILDREN are raised—until I see where *I* was raised.

"Gambol, you look very sad."

"It's about the CHILDREN and getting pregnant. If I am sterile, it would be a great loss to me. But Rogar, I don't think I am."

"Why not?"

"It's something I must not tell you."

She looked still more unhappy.

I took her hand, led her behind some artificial trees, and put my arms around her.

She is broader than I am, but for the first time her size did not make me feel small; her size made me feel strong.

I've been ashamed of *my* body, too. I have not wanted to write about it in my Journal—that I am such a small man, five feet four inches, a full six inches shorter than I'm supposed to be. It is difficult for me to believe any woman can let herself be seen with me without embarrassment.

"I cannot believe you want me," this lovely woman says. "Twenty-eight years in hiding—hidden forever, I was sure."

We held and held, and I could feel our bodies relaxing.

[59]

I want to be at ease with her pain, as well as mine.

We sat down again, this time upon a cushion of artificial grass.

"Tell me things, Rogar."

"What things?"

"About you. Things I don't know. I feel so naked with you now, I need to know more and more about you. No, that is unfair. You should say only what you want to say. You need tell me nothing."

She smiled, pleased to have arrived again at this Independence of hers.

"I feel myself coming alive with you and with my Journal," I said.

"Your Journal? You record your Private Self? Not just history, but Yourself?"

"That's why my Great Book Hallucination means so much to me. I am a writer, and all of my life I've been reading a Great Book that lives inside me, but I can never recall it when I'm awake."

"I understand that so well, Rogar."

"Do you have a Vision?"

"We cannot hope for everything at once," she said sadly.

"What do you mean?"

She would not answer.

"You'll be in my Journal," I said. "But that's promising to include you in a treasonous conspiracy. Perhaps I should not write about you."

"You have to put me in your Journal. I'm in your life."

"Aren't you afraid?"

"That wouldn't matter. It's your Journal, and you have to be the one to determine what goes into your Journal."

"It's *your* life."

"No, your words inside your Journal are all yours, just as my thoughts inside my body are all mine."

"I love your body. I want you without the Bag!"

I believe her face trembled, as on the mountain when I first touched her.

"I am not yet ready to be transformed," she said.

"I have such power with you?"

"You have great power, Rogar."

Neither of us spoke for several minutes.

"What are you thinking?" she asked me after a while. "There's something new on your face."

"I'm beginning to see why I needed you this morning. And it's odd, but it was on your mind too in a way. Something about the Great Jews, something about reading the Bible stories has made me want to visit the Zoo and to think about the blacks."

"I dislike looking at the blacks."

A dangerous thing to say, and I looked up automatically. No one embarrasses himself by criticizing the black confinement in the Zoo. The blacks are there to be cared for and enjoyed. They live in a rather large and splendid area of Washington, D.C., the old National Zoo and much of the Rock Creek Park, all contained within electronic barriers.

This is not supposed to be a racial policy, since

[61]

ancestry and general racial characteristics are not stigmatizing. It is simply a color policy: anyone with a Skin Reading of 2-Plus Niger Units on a Niger Counter is used for medical experimentation if found outside the Zoo. And so it's said that the Zoo is really a sanctuary for dark people.

I recall my nightmare from the morning. During an Attitude Check, an Official took out his Niger Counter and found my face darker than 2-Plus.

5th Entry

"As much as I hate this place," Gambol said, "seeing the blacks in the Zoo always makes me think."

"Why?"

"Their different color makes me aware how separate they are from us. And that forces me to face how little separateness we have in NOW America . . . Rogar, once a black man came as close as he could to me across the barriers—less than a hundred feet—and when I looked at him, I felt, 'That's a man!' That never happens to me in NOW America."

I can understand the rage of Oldtime white men against the black men.

Gambol read my expression and said, "Sometimes when I look into your face, I feel scared and uncertain for you. Rogar, do you really know what it means to be a separate person?"

I turned my attention to a place in the distance where I could make out a group of small black children inside the Zoo. A few years ago they would have been begging from the whites, running up and down behind the barriers doing handstands and somersaults while the whites rewarded them by throwing candy-smeared rocks across the barriers. The children would dodge these sticky missiles and then scramble like crazy to suck a sweet rock.

The child who could stand closest to the missile without being struck down by it had the best chance to grab the booty. Hence the expression, "standing like a hungry nigger child."

But something has happened inside the Zoo, and hardly any blacks "suck candied rock" any more. This had led some of my fellow Bureaucrats to complain, "They don't appreciate anything we do for them. After all, they couldn't possibly survive in there without us."

There are other ominous activities going on in the Zoo, marching and parading about with much shouting of orders, as if the Zoo penguins had suddenly begun to organize. Indeed, discussing the activities of blacks takes up a great deal of Dynamo energy at lunch and at parties. As a topic, they are second only to Taking Pleasure and Bagging Good Lays.

But there is little chance the Blacks could break out in any numbers from behind the barriers. Their food is shipped in to them on a Conveyor Belt which returns, empty, through a poisonous bath. And if a black man could nonetheless escape, what could he find for himself in white America?

Gambol and I disembarked in front of the Official

[64]

History, and I realized that I had always avoided studying this one.

I glanced around to make sure that no Official was nearby to notice that I was reading instead of Imprinting. Then I began:

A COMPLETE HISTORY
OF
THE BLACK CONSPIRACY

The Black Conspiracy against America dates from the days when African chieftains conspired to sell their fiercest neighbors to white slavers—thereby ridding themselves of these competitors and enabling them to plant a fifth column of Super Blacks within white America. Survival of the Fittest was furthered by transport in coffinlike slave ships, by the rigors of slavery itself, by deliberate breeding practices on slave farms, by the hard life of Slum Ghettos, and, finally, by the disproportionate numbers subjected to front-line duty in America's many wars. Ultimately, their persecution produced among blacks emotional ties of such distinction that even the whites envied them for their "soul." Thus while White America went on proliferating without regard for its racial stock, Black America was toughened and matured by stresses seldom known to man. A race of Super Blacks was produced.

Despite predictions of disaster from the Great Watchful Majority, an aging Supreme Court then granted the blacks an almost imperceptible degree of equality. Immediately they took advantage. Within a short time, black giants—some more than seven feet tall—were dominating every major sport, even as smaller black men of uncommon talents had taken over the

[65]

entertainment industry. In art and in politics, they began to make their "black mark" upon the nation. But it was sexual pride that finally brought the black and white into armed conflict, for when the sexual barriers were at last brought down, it was discovered that black men and black women almost without exception preferred each other to white people.

It took nearly a year of warfare to pen the Super Blacks up within the Zoos all over America.

Even in the Zoo today you will see how black people of all ages and sexes seem to derive an uncommon spontaneous pleasure from each other's company. You will also see that the black man continues to derive a satisfaction from competition that has long passed away in NOW America; and if you look carefully, you will note a certain physical hypertrophy that speaks of sexual hyperpotency. Nor must the black man's cunning be overlooked. He is an animal who aspires, perspires, and conspires.

Hence the expression "nigger" has come to mean anyone who strives too hard and who has an unfair competitive advantage through Genetic Endowment and Natural Selection.

"I don't suppose it's so bad in there," Gambol said at last. "With Weather Control they don't need any clothes, they get plenty of food and medicine, and they're left alone to organize and entertain themselves. They have natural trees and greenery all around them in Rock Creek Park, and they seem to play a lot more than we do. And Rogar, I've noticed some of them doing things that look like arts and crafts. The last time I was here, one fellow in the trees seemed to be sketching the white people. It doesn't sound like a bad place for an artist!" she said with an enthusiasm I didn't understand.

[66]

"If I were an artist, I wouldn't want to flee into the Zoo," I said. "That's what the government would *want* me to do."

"I've heard that illicit lovers sometimes flee into the Zoo when they've been caught Without the Bag," said Gambol. "And maybe pregnant women, too."

I wonder if I would rather be Capped, or forced to flee into the Zoo? Capping, with its remote-control devices and a governor to dampen the emotions, seems far worse—a loss of something I cannot name, something to do with myself and Gambol.

Hearing laughter, we turned and waved to a young black couple running like a pair of sleek deer. The man stopped and raised his hand over his head in a fist, probably a sexual sign, and when I turned to Gambol she had raised her fist in a return salute. Then we both glanced quickly around. No one was in sight.

The black couple was gone, too.

"On our way out, let's look at the Simulated Ghetto," I said.

And then it occurred to me—ghettos were originally for Jews! A place for any kind of Super People? No wonder I've been afraid to examine Black History.

The Simulated Ghetto was a couple of hundred yards long and fifty feet deep, with several levels of Conveyors moving in front of it and numerous Electronic Screens filled with history and data.

The exhibit displayed one five-story tenement with a cutaway front and several smaller houses with cutaway walls. The plastic black models, many performing simple

[67]

motions, looked almost alive. There were fat women with great arms and bellies, heavily muscled men, skinny children, mangy dogs, a few cats, and some cruel-looking squirrel-like animals with hairless tails and pointed faces.

The Official History screens offered facts and figures about the numbers of people crammed into these spaces, the pre-Weather Control conditions which left them without heat in the winter and without air conditioning in the summer, the collapsing ceilings and broken-down plumbing, the lack of general sanitation, medical care, education, jobs. There were special notes on where to look for garbage strewn about, unconscious drunks, sick drug addicts, and the like.

The human interaction simulations were impressive. On one corner a young black boy was lying on the pavement bleeding and writhing while two white police-men stood above him rhythmically raising their clubs up and down, up and down. The movement was jerky, but otherwise quite convincing. By a doorstep, two little mechanical black children were poking a short stick at one of the animals with a hairless tail. Backed into a corner, it was baring its teeth. A third little black boy was holding a red finger that had been bitten.

On another step an elderly woman with a brightly dressed little girl was trying to climb over the heaving body of a drunken man upon the steps. Broken glass and quart bottles lay around.

A man was urinating against a wall.

Near a lamppost a small black child was being held

up at knifepoint by two larger black children. A few steps away, a policeman, this time black, was taking money from a black man.

On a far corner, an elderly black man was begging change from a well-dressed white man. Close by, a black youngster was smashing the window of a car.

The view through one cutaway wall showed five little children trying to sleep on a floor while a man and woman were doing something on the room's one old mattress. Two children were also asleep on the mattress.

"Gambol," I said, "this is ridiculous! It's obviously been set up to make us think the Zoo isn't so bad by comparison. No one, not even a Super Black, could have survived growing up in a place like that. And no one, not the most callous Oldtime White, could have tolerated its existence."

I backed away with a renewed conviction that I could never trust a word of Official History.

6th Entry

Here it is! My uncensored history of the Hebrew Disease in America, a preliminary report put together from my secret research. I am afraid that it may be heavily contaminated with the lies of Official History, but I have begun to realize that to understand myself I must learn *as much as possible* about the Jews and the origins of the Disease.

Within a matter of months after our winning of the Good War, a malaise began settling upon the land. At a time when all were expected to celebrate the Total Victory with unrestrained joy, people instead became irritable, complained of many symptoms in their heads and bodies, and sometimes withdrew into a stupor that ended inexorably in death. If anywhere in the nation a man or woman awoke feeling heavy in his head, sluggish in his bowels and limbs, or simply saddened in his mood, he could not be certain that he would see the end of the day.

Paranoids within the citizenry accused the Military of unleashing so-called dirty bombs in the war, and diagnosed the malaise as radiation sickness. But to the average American it looked as though a Plague of Unhappiness was upon the land; a communicable disease, with tears as its primary symptom. Tearful people were stoned to death by the thousands, and many thousands more were blinded by mutilating operations on their tear ducts. Many politicians picked up the theme in their slogans: "Happiness is a public health responsibility," or "The government owes you your happiness."

Happiness Groups and Joy Groups began to abound. Every morning and every evening, at work and at home, people gathered in Groups. Weekend marathons, week-long Grouper retreats, and even two-month Grouper Devotions in Grouper Centers ushered in the nation's newest form of worship.

America was meanwhile dismayed by the surfacing of youthful Radicals who self-righteously proclaimed that the Victorious nation deserved to collapse in GUILT, SHAME, and ANXIETY. Blaming their leaders and their parents, they urged self-determination and reparations for the people of the Conquered Lands.

To advocate *any* foreign policy was ridiculed by most Americans as an anachronism, for with worldwide power in our hands, all policy became domestic policy. At any rate, the Radicals, who were found to be infiltrated by Hebrew Agent-Priests, fell victim to the Great Purges—a veritable bloodbath of Jewish sons and daughters.

[72]

The Liberals, who, in many cases, were parents to the Radicals, were not overly preoccupied with the loss of their children through war or through purge, for they agreed with the great majority that the Victory was worth it. They argued heatedly that the GUILT and SHAME could be cured by announcing to the People that the Victory was not total: that another nation existed nearly unharmed, armed and defiant but contained. Israel seemed the logical choice for this rumor, since its military feats and capacity for survival were already legendary among Americans, and because it would be easy to unite America in opposition to mankind's COMMON ENEMY, the Jew.

The logic of the Liberals had one inescapable flaw—while the belief in Israel's survival might relieve America's Guilt and Shame, fear of her infamous acts of retaliation would make the nation's Gentiles "as anxious as Arabs."

The Liberal faction itself was riddled with Jews, but no purge was necessary. They were so ill with the Hebrew Disease that they simply wasted away and died from their own excessive Guilt, Shame, and Anxiety.

A truly unique salvation was preached by the new Church of Abused Mankind. When even our Total Victory was spoiled by the Disease, the Church of Abused Mankind declared that an honest analysis of all history allowed for only one interpretation:

GOD IS JEWISH
and
HE is *against* MANKIND!

[73]

God was declared the ULTIMATE ENEMY, and America was urged to mobilize its scientific energy against Him.

Flush with our Victory in the Good War, some Americans were willing to take on God Himself, until they realized that even if we won against the Ultimate Enemy, we could never *prove* our Victory. We would become "winners without a Trophy."

With the collapse of the Church of Abused Mankind, religion came to an end as a serious force within American life. The purges and the wasting effects of the Disease had virtually wiped out the political power of the Jews; the blacks were penned up within the Zoos; and though I cannot yet trace in detail the demise of three minority parties—the Women, the Human Beings, and the People—it is apparent that by the sixth decade After the Good War political power had fallen into the hands of the Leftover American. His party, the Great Watchful Majority, had survived it all in silence, and had at last become *the* party of the nation.

From those of vintage American stock to those who were more newly seasoned, these Leftover Americans had one thing in common: all denied any awareness of Guilt, Shame, or Anxiety within themselves. Their motto became "No Jewish Tears run in our ducts."

Establishment Science now supported the Party by declaring the Contagion to be a true biologic illness with mental and physical symptoms, a "social disease" that had tormented mankind for centuries, breaking out in periodic epidemics but always smoldering, endemic to

[74]

the earth and to men. And the disease was given its proper name: the *Hebrew Disease,* GUILT, SHAME, and ANXIETY.

The vector of this disease? Jewish tears, of course— those colorless, odorless, nearly tasteless drops. One drop upon a sugar cube was known to cause serious derangements; several drops might throw the victim into an incurable psychosis. Radical Hebrew youths were known to flaunt their dependence upon these Tear-drops, while even among their parents there was evidence of a Liberal indulgence. And how easily could Israeli Agent-Priests have deposited whole dropperfuls into our water supplies before the destruction of Israel in the Good War! Hence the terror of SPREADING TEARS still grips the people. And hence the Grouper Tenth Commandment, "Thou Shalt Not SPREAD TEARS."

The Jews had actually begun to look upon them-selves as Diseased long before the remainder of America caught on. As early as the Twentieth Century, a popular Jewish novelist had ridiculed the Jewish character and described it as a psychiatric "Complaint," traceable to a perverted family life. That this book lacked any understanding of the politics of the Hebrew Disease tells us the extent to which the Jewish Intellectual had become alienated from his own intellect.

Increasing fear and prejudice against the Jews broke out into more open political anti-Semitism in the fourth decade After the Good War with the disclosure of the Lessinger Plot of the late Twentieth Century. This man

[75]

Lessinger, it was learned, had corrupted one of the purest and most patriotic Presidents in the history of the land, and had managed to transform him into a traitor who betrayed the nation to international communism. This was not the first time in history that a Jew had seduced the leadership of a great Empire. Egypt had its Joseph, and Spain and Germany had theirs. As in each case, the only solution was expulsion or extermination.

Despite this, the Jews themselves were dealt with as humanely as possible. They were offered the alternative of painless sterilization or death by medical experimentation. And, of course, Capping always loomed in the background.

Lacking reliable records, I can only surmise why the Jews apparently mounted no significant resistance. The 152 years of Israel's national revival Before the Good War were the most fear-free in four thousand or more years of Jewish history and the presumed loss of Israel in the Good War may have destroyed their morale. More important, the Jewish Establishment's unabashed celebration of America's Victory may have shattered the American Jew's sense of identity as a worldwide people, thus preparing him to accept promises of personal survival in exchange for sterilization and the death of the race. To fight for unborn generations is far more difficult than to fight for one's own survival, and the betrayal of Israel may have made the challenge too demanding.

[76]

As in Nazi Germany, their high degree of assimilation must have also made it hard for Establishment Jews to believe what was happening in America, much as their material prosperity must have made it impossible to sacrifice all in armed resistance. Leftist Jewry, militant in everything except the defense of Jews, actually set itself up for liquidation in the most amazing fashion. Seeking to find an Israeli-like solution for themselves in America, many so-called Buberites had established Communes and Kibbutzim in and around major cities. When it was time to round up Jews, it was then a simple matter for the authorities to ring these Buberite settlements with barbed wire and land mines, turning them into mini-concentration camps within a matter of hours.

Even after all the Jews in the nation had been gathered together behind barbed wire, Leftist and Establishment Jews alike anticipated their release as Clean Jews after a period of isolation, patriotic indoctrination, and treatment. Hence to describe anyone who fails to learn from history, I offer this expression: "He thinks like a Jew."

Strange that these Jewish People were the descendants of the first great National Freedom Fighters—the one people to free itself from servitude to the Greek Empire and to rebel repeatedly against the Roman Empire until the Romans celebrated their devastation as the crowning glory of their military history. Stranger still that only two centuries earlier, in 1948, militant

[77]

Jews had liberated themselves in a war against over-whelming odds—the combined Arab nations and their British military advisers.

In the ancient tradition of the Maccabees and the Zealots, and the Twentieth-century tradition of the Israeli Irgun and the American Hebrew Defense League, one small group of Jewish Freedom Fighters did struggle against annihilation with organized terror and guerrilla warfare. But as in the past, they met more effective resistance from their own assimilated leaders than from the enemy. They were turned in by their own Leftist and Liberal Establishment and easily wiped out.

There is ample evidence that the Great Watchful Majority of Leftover Americans accepted and collabo-rated in the fate of the Jews. The precedent had been set when the black man had been confined, and it was deeply resented that the blacks' few white sympathizers had been Jews. Hitler's earlier annihilation of millions of Jews also made America's policies seem benign by comparison. In America every docile Jew was at least allowed to live out his sterile lifetime. Collaborating Jews could boast, "It *didn't* happen here."

Nor did the issue of sterilization stir up much sym-pathy among any Americans, most of whom had sought it for themselves as a personal means of birth control. The nation was already well on its way toward the reforms which would do away with the family as a unit of reproduction. In fighting and dying for their genetic preservation, the Jews would have been taking up a cause no ordinary American would take up for himself.

[78]

In truth, the Jews' fate differed hardly at all from that of the average American.

Probably the Jews' only hope lay in throwing in their lot with the blacks at the very start of the black resistance, but they were each divided from the other by those very prejudices that turned all America against them both. At any rate, in this the second century After the Good War, there are no known Jews and no known Jewish offspring surviving in America, and their potential allies, the blacks, are never seen outside the Zoo.

But if the Jews themselves are no longer a threat, why must we yet struggle so desperately against a recurrence of the Hebrew Disease? Is the genetic taint ineradicable? Is the Disease itself still endemic to the American population? Or does Israel still exist, spreading its Plague across the ocean?

Perhaps the Church of Abused Mankind touched upon the answer. Perhaps God Himself—that same God who visited the Disease so cruelly upon the Hebrews—is indeed THE ULTIMATE ENEMY.

Must America eventually confront this ULTIMATE ENEMY? And if so, what is the nature of His threat?

7th Entry

Below me the city is a vast surface made almost flat by the lack of anything outstanding. Subtle variations in depth and shading as one Stack of Cubes blends into another turn it into an immense cubist contour map layered upon the remains of Oldtime Washington, D.C. Only the giant slender Needles break the monotony.

I eased my Bubble down on Gambol's Stack of Cubes and took the chute down to the second tier of ten stories.

Gambol threw great bear arms around me and held me crushed tight; then she set me away from her. "I feel ready to show you something."

She unsnapped the front of her Pleasure Pack to disclose a small audiovisual outfit with a tiny lens.

"I take videotapes," she explained, "and then, well, I bring them home . . . and then I watch them and . . ."

I prepared myself for anything.

"Rogar . . ."

"Yes?"

"I study them, the voices, the faces, the movements, and, Rogar, I make paintings of people."

Only a historian would know what she was talking about. In the Twentieth Century the artist had severed himself from his true energy source as the interpreter of mankind and nature, and instead had become the interpreter of art. Artist and critic had become one, and art had died.

Soft golden light was glowing in a great aura around Gambol's cheeks. Her brown eyes had become amber wafers.

She pulled an enormous canvas from the wall slot closet and stuck it up against an expanse of white wall. It was a portrait.

My face looked rugged and alive, a little strained around the eyes but gentle; my tangled hair grew like wild grass over my forehead and ears. Deep-set eyes, green and brown with teardrop spokes of orange, looked back at me. And my mouth was not at all so hard as I had supposed. Then I realized: Gambol had painted me as I drew tenderly away after a kiss.

She brought in two smaller paintings and leaned them against the wall. The first was an Official staring at the back of a man standing in Free-Association Posture. From the wild hair, thick neck, and bulled shoulders, it was me. The second painting showed the Official, full face, staring out at us. At us? At Gambol, I could tell, from the lust in his eyes and mouth, a fearful look, a leer at someone he could not understand.

I took a small present for her from behind my

Pleasure Pack—some fragments of Revolutionary Documents, including the one that begins, "We hold these truths . . ." I inserted a capsule in her Q Tube and, for the first time, played sections of my Journal for her.

After dinner we wrestled flesh to flesh on the floor, and Gambol tried to tumble me over, usually collapsing in a great heap. Once when I got up, she charged squarely into me from behind and fell down again. I am built something like the stump of a middle-sized tree. But when she attacked me with tickles, we both broke into helpless giggles, and when she looked at me with love, this tree stump turned into a glowing, melting candle of a man.

She drew herself down to the floor with me and we sat knee to knee, leaning across our laps, kissing and playing tongue to tongue and toying with our bodies.

We rested for a while and then I found myself collecting my thoughts and taking notes for a new Journal entry. Never before had I written in front of anyone.

When I looked up Gambol had clothes on!—a thin white shirt splattered as if a rainbow had shattered and showered upon her, and a pair of blue, body-tight pants covered with drippings and the prints of many hand-wipings. The comical clownish colors made her beauty more profound.

I watched her paint for many minutes, then I went to work on my Journal. Thus began the most peaceful several hours of my life.

[83]

8th Entry

"Rogar, it's not safe for me to call you right now, so listen carefully." Gambol spoke to me from my home Q Tube the next morning. "There was something going on at the Office today. My Boss has been talking about the biological inferiority of women, and today he asked if I would give him *one last chance* to Bag me."

"Just a horny Dynamo."

"He warned me to show up at work on time tomorrow morning."

"They wouldn't tip their hand so easily."

"Rogar, an Official was in to see me today. He put me through a Mood Evaluation and asked questions about my sex life."

"Let me come see you. No, let me meet you somewhere."

"Absolutely not!"

"But we could ..." Could what? Flee to an imagined Israel? Flee into the Zoo?

"I have to face tomorrow alone, Rogar. But I wanted you to know in case I disappear."

"Gambol!"

"Just wait for me at America's Most Proud Erection at noon. By then I should know what's going on."

"But if you don't show up?"

"Goodbye, Rogar." Her face disappeared from the Q Tube.

I may never see her again.

Or she may be Capped the next time I see her.

Gambol!

Your face, your tender open face. Why haven't I told you how beautiful you are?

Beautiful? That overweight, lumbering woman who won't let me Bag her? And she's not even an O.B.P.!

There, I feel much better: a soothing blank, a calm void with no one in it.

In a nation full of Cocksuckers, Playgirls, and Good Lays, in a nation full of women dying to become Dependents, I don't need to do this to myself over anyone.

But my heart is beating like a kettledrum.

Slow down!

Her face glows before my eyes again and I see my life ahead of me: I see it with Gambol, and I see it without Gambol—

I stretch out and think about her—about how it feels to be Bubble-close to her, how it feels to talk with her and listen to her, how it feels when she asks a single question that straightens out all my twisted thinking, how it feels to put my hand inside her, how it feels to

[86]

smell her. I think about how it will feel to make love with her *Without the Bag.*

The Conveyor was moving toward America's Most Proud Erection, that Day-glo missile and balls, and I could see the small park where Gambol would meet me.

As I stepped off there were no Officials in sight.

A large red bird dipped its beak into the sparkling-burgundy foam of the fountain, turned, saw me, and flew off. It's a rare experience nowadays, this meeting between bird and man within the megalopolis.

I see Gambol!

She is standing tall and proud, her hair blowing about her head as the Conveyor pulls her through a gentle breeze, then striding toward me.

We do not touch.

"What's happened?" I ask her.

"They made me an Official Beautiful Person this morning. That's what all the crap was about."

"Then you're safe. We're both still safe!"

But her fists were clenched at her sides.

"My Boss called us together and gave me the O.B.P. Certificate and made sexual jokes about my figure and my breasts and what a Lay I'd become."

"It sounds no different from any other O.B.P. awarding. And you do look wonderful."

Her features tightened and squinted with contained feelings; her whole face took on new angularity. Gone was the soft, absorbing woman.

[87]

"I told them they could use their O.B.P. Certificate to wrap up their cunt liners and their Love Bags and shove the whole mess. I told them NOW is no damn better than any other time for women. Then I walked out on their little ceremony."

"No one came after you to Check you?"

"I waited alone in my office for about an hour."

Her woman's face was firm and strong, flush with color and full with feelings.

"Rogar, there's no telling when or how they might descend upon you or me. It might be tomorrow, or they might observe us for months. Or they might not even worry about me—men are supposed to be more dangerous than women. I've risked you by standing up for myself."

"You told me that my Journal and my life are my own to do with as I choose."

Her face softened, and she put her warm hands upon my shoulders and looked at me.

Gambol and I were alone on our mountain, the first time we had dared to Blow Off together since her refusal to become an O.B.P. My Bubble sat glistening on the pad, the only one in sight except for those gliding silently through the rising mists of the Shenandoah Valley.

"Rogar, there's something else I want to tell you. I went Into the Bag the other night with someone I met at a Pleasure Party."

I felt the sickness in my stomach.

"I frightened him right out of his Bag," she said in hushed tones. "I must have made a sound—a sound meant for you. He popped right out of the Bag and wouldn't have anything more to do with me."

"Here, Gambol, sit down with me." I spread out a plastic blanket amid a clump of low evergreens. "You were too much for him, that's all."

"Rogar, you'll listen to me, even about this?"

"I'll listen."

"That's all there was. My feelings for you are growing so strong that I had to do it. I miss you when we're apart, Rogar, and that's never happened to me before."

My body was again under my command.

"I haven't Bagged a Playgirl in months," I told her. "And being with My Girl is like lying down with death itself. But at least I can reduce my tensions with My Girl."

"I only have needs for *you,*" Gambol blurted out. "And all the pleasure in the world isn't going to satisfy them."

"Gambol, here, let me hold you."

I enfolded her for a few moments, wrapping her body in mine; legs on legs, thighs on thighs, belly on belly. Then we lay on our backs and stared up into the blue sky.

"You don't mind that I need My Girl?" I asked her.

"Needing without wanting is something that's been done to you," she said.

My pike popped from my Ball Pack, and she was

[89]

already reaching for me, both hands around me, and there was pike to spare.

"Let me Bag you," I begged. "Please. It'll be so much better with me. I'm not afraid of your feelings."

She took her hands from my pike. "I don't know what I want."

I sat up on the crushed grass and crinkly plastic, staring in despair at the longest pike I'd ever poked, then lay down beside her and kissed through her hair and into her ear. Then pressing my face into the grass, I bit into the ground and seized the roots in my teeth. The roots! And then I put my mouth to Gambol's thighs, and I did what would disgust any NOW man—I sucked her root hairs and her cunt.

"No! No! No! No!" As she screamed, she was pulling on my penis, my penis now too flaccid to be called a pike, "No! No!" and she was shuddering beneath my face, her belly rising, falling, her thighs shaking, lifting my head, crushing my head, suffocating me; and I lap her up and draw in her smells, evil smells, evil odors, dirty odors; and I drive my face and then my tongue into her, wanting to tell her, "I love your body! I love YOU."

How I wanted to believe it was good!

"No!" She shouts once more, her body rigid before climax; then she suddenly sits erect, her strong hands yanking my hair to straighten me up.

We are both panting, and my face is wet with her.

Never has this NOW man felt so crippled. And never has a woman looked at me with such great bewildered love-filled eyes.

[90]

I am confused beyond saving.

I was still sitting cross-legged staring down into my unsatisfied lap when we heard the sound of heavy footsteps crashing through the underbrush.

Gambol sat up, and I jumped to my feet to face the man charging toward us from the trees.

Beyond him, his Official Bubble stood beside ours on the Pad.

"I saw you! I saw you!" he screamed. "Identify yourselves!"

My voice shook as I announced with all the authority I could summon, "I am T. E. P. Rogar, O.B., O.B.P., NAMS, Chief Historian, Oldtime Twentieth Century."

"What? What? A Bureaucrat groveling between a woman's legs? Sucking out the filth from her body?"

He turned to Gambol. "And *you?*"

"J. A. R. D. Gambol, O.B., NAMS, Chief Psychologist for Female Wishfulfillment."

"A ranking female psychologist, letting a Dynamo grovel like a filthy pig in the sty of your body? Pig!" He screamed and waved his binoculars at her. Then he spat, a glob of saliva splattering upon her belly.

I reached down and picked up a rock.

The rock feels heavy enough to crush his skull.

"Go ahead, do your Angry Thing," he said. "Throw it at a tree, you'll feel better."

This will be the first time I have struck a man.

"Rogar, no!"

But I am moving toward him with the rock.

[91]

"What are you doing? You can't hit an Official. No one kills Officials any more. No one Kills Because the Killing's Done and We've Done It All." He stutters as he repeats the Good War slogan.

Gambol touches my arm. Not restraint, not panic—tenderness. Even now, tenderness! And tears are running down her face, great frightened tears.

"You're maniacs!" He shrieks. "SPREADING TEARS! Threatening an Official! Degenerates! Maniacs! Jews! And you, YOU"—he shakes his binoculars at Gambol—"What kind of *thing* are you?"

I raise the rock.

"Rogar, no." She touches my arm again. "Not for me. Don't kill him for me."

Now the man is running, stumbling through the underbrush and trees; falling, getting up, fleeing up the hill toward the Bubble Pad. He is carrying our lives away with him.

I could overtake him, but I stand beside Gambol and watch, wondering how long it will take him to regain his senses and send someone after us. And my final thought is not for me, or for Gambol, but for my work. I will never finish my Journal.

There's an enormous roar as his Official Bubble leaps into the air amid the bursts of its emergency take-off rockets. It flips over and out of control, its stabilizer rockets firing out of synchrony!

We watched him tumbling end over end in a long trajectory, wobbling through the sky like a sputtering firecracker. He smashed into the mountainside and in seconds he had disappeared in a great orange burst, followed by a plume of flame and smoke that rose into the sky. We watched the burning rocket fuel spread slowly over half an acre or more, wiping out the forest, the smashed Bubble, and the remains of its pilot.

We walked quickly but without panic toward the Pad and Blew Off in my Bubble.

As much as I wanted to hurry, I was glad that unofficial Bubbles are not equipped with auxiliary rockets.

I headed west over the valley to return roundabout to Washington, and within moments we were beyond the mountain range. The sun sent the round purple shadow of our Bubble chasing along the foothills beside us. I felt isolated, like an astronaut watching his sick purple earth grow cold and dark and dead beneath him.

I told her what she already knew: "A man is dead because we're alive. The life in us killed him." I turned my head and squinted into the burning sun.

We remained silent until we landed on the Pad atop Gambol's Stack of Cubes.

"I'd better not stay here with you tonight, Gambol. I'll call you in the morning."

"No, Rogar. I don't want us to see each other for a while."

I felt like a man injured and afraid to know the extent of his injury.

"But why? Because they might be watching us?"

She didn't answer.

"Tell me!"

[93]

"I think we shouldn't see each other for a while. That's all."

"What are you talking about?"

"I don't know for how long. One of us will have to decide and call the other."

"Then I'll call you tomorrow."

"No, please, not for a long time."

"Are you afraid we'll be accused of murder?"

"Yes, of course."

"But that's not the reason. Is it?"

"The reason has to do with my feelings and my fears, and that's all I can tell you."

She kissed me warmly, but her face felt cold against mine.

"There is something I wanted to give you today, Rogar, something I found in the Female Archive a long time ago. You can put it in your Journal if you want, but mostly I want you to read it for yourself and for me."

She took a capsule from within her Pleasure Pack, handed it to me, and said, "Good night." Then she left me alone upon the Pad.

It was many minutes before I could collect myself sufficiently to take off.

Here is the material Gambol left with me.

HUMAN BEINGS!

Human Beings in hiding throughout America, this is our history. Be proud! Human Beings of the future, this is your history, too. Read it and respond! Awaken to our cry, Liberty and Love!

In the first decades After the Good War, the growing Liberation of Women augured well for the coming of Human Beings. Like the Blacks and the Jews before their disasters, the Women had won places for themselves in nearly every field of competition. They already dominated those requiring higher sensibilities and abstract reasoning: the arts, mathematics, and the pure sciences.

But while the Women were able to liberate themselves to compete, they still remained slaves to the one need that can never know healthy gratification—the need for approval from others. The need for the respect of men still hung about their necks like a stone.

Meanwhile, besieged on all sides by Blacks, Jews, and Women, the Leftover Male American reacted to the Women's Movement with increasing ridicule and resentment. In frustration, the most militant feminists, the Furies, resorted to terrorist bombings and assassinations in their demand for respect. Even the simultaneous assassination of two males on the Supreme Court and three in the President's Cabinet, accompanied by demands for the appointment of Furious Women to fill the vacancies, failed to elicit the respect with which Americans traditionally crown almost any terrorist activity. If anything, feminist extremism earned increasing ridicule, as if it proved the depravity of any Woman's wish for equality.

Then the appearance of the Sweethearts rent the Women's Movement. "Tenderness, not Terror," the Sweethearts cried, as they demanded nothing, but offered love. Respect, they insisted, was a second-rate masculine substitute for love; and love, they believed, was the essence of womanhood.

Though rape had been nearly wiped out by retaliatory castrations and lynchings engineered by Furious Women, the Sweethearts now walked undefended and alone throughout the cities at all hours, inviting encounters and offering tenderness to any man who

[95]

wanted it. Attempted rapes were turned into seductions, and a whole new era of nocturnal city life was inaugurated.

American males applauded this innovation in Women's Liberation, and the "Sweettarts," as men called them, were openly feted by the most diehard male elitists. But the honeymoon was short-lived, as men began to find this uncompromised sweetness more unsettling than any Furious threat. Stag parties with Sweethearts turned into binges, the men throwing themselves upon each other in drunken embraces. More and more frequently Sweethearts were found dead and unspeakably mutilated in their homes and on the streets. The Male Media tried to blame these atrocities upon the Furies, who did vacillate between protecting the Sweethearts and condemning them; but it soon became undeniable that the atrocities were caused by something that can only be called Male Sadism.

Why should Male Sadism be directed against the Sweethearts? Surely the Furies were a more fitting target than the hapless Sweethearts, who were trained to respond lovingly to the most vicious abuser. "Tenderness, not Torture," they would whisper through broken teeth, cracked lips, and torn tongues; and most kept their vows until death, offering love even as their tormenters amputated and tore out their female organs.

We owe our understanding of Male Sadism to those few Sweethearts who were saved from death. They reported uniformly that they had been tortured with increasing cruelty as long as they kept responding with tenderness and understanding—only to be released and even treated kindly, once they gave in and vented hate and rage upon their tormentors. Thus maimed in spirit as well as in body, these surviving Sweethearts testified to the goal of Male Sadism.

As long as the Women's Movement was confined to the Furies and the Sweethearts, male resistance in general remained sporadic and even apathetic. It was

[96]

limited largely to ridicule and these occasional atrocities. Then, in the third decade After the Good War, we
Human Beings were first heard from, voicing our
extraordinary motto: "We fight like men and love like
women!" Tough and Tender as required, we taught
ourselves to fight defensively when necessary and yet to
love with total vulnerability whenever possible.

We abandoned that misguided need for the respect
of men. We even put aside that more worthy goal, to
love men. Instead we began where human beings must
begin, with respect and love for ourselves. Soon we
discovered that even our own motto had been born of
corruption, and that neither sex had more potential to
fight or to love. "We fight and love like Human Beings,"
was all we need say.

We fully intended to be a mixed group, females and
males, but male liberation remained as sluggish as ever,
so that most of our new recruits continued to come
through defections from the Furies and the Sweethearts.
Within a few years, nearly all the Human Beings in
America were women.

As we grew in number and in strength, a peculiar
mental paralysis overcame Male America. Millions of
words were written and spoken by the Male Media
explaining how all female Human Beings were either
Furies, Sweethearts, or Jewish Radicals in disguise.
Hardly a man in the population believed *anyone* could
be a Human Being, least of all a woman!

Sadistic male assaults continued against the Sweet-
hearts, but by now both the Furies and the Human
Beings were so adept at self-defense that hostile males
kept their distance. A joke made the rounds of Male
Chauvinist Clubs: "Sadists go after Sweethearts, and
Masochists go after Furies, but none of us go after
Human Beings." Only a Human Being would have
anything to do with another Human Being.

We Human Beings suffered painfully from our
isolation in America, and most of us were periodically

[97]

overwhelmed with severe symptoms of the Hebrew Disease: acute loneliness mixed with fits of depression, confusion, anxiety, self-hate, and rage. So frequently were we overcome that many men took the attitude that Women, not Jews, were the source of the Hebrew Disease.

Because so many of us eventually succumbed to the Disease in middle life, Official Male Psychiatry most often called our problem "Involutional Depression" or "Involutional Paranoia," to suggest that it grew "naturally" out of our later years.

Psychiatry found endless explanations for our problems, most of them biological, as if our aging female bodies gave off toxins; and these explanations invariably ignored the facts of our lives. But whatever the presumed cause or the current name of our "disease," we were inevitably treated in the same way: exhortations to return to more appropriate female activities, followed by physical enforcement through drugs, Pleasure Hospitalization, and Capping. Not even an experienced Human Being could withstand these technological assaults. She would learn to hide whatever feeling had survived the various therapies, and of course she would be unable to fight for herself or to give herself in love. Needless to say, she was lost to the ranks of the Human Beings.

We Human Beings, knowing that the problem came from trying to be a Whole Person in America, called it "Human Being Anguish," or simply, "Human Anguish." The world around us was so Hostile and Unloving that hardly any woman could maintain herself—defending herself from unending humiliation while seeking for the opportunity to love with all her heart. We found in fact that the most devoted Human Beings among us were the most vunerable.

When one of us was struck down, we did not institute "treatments," nor did we degrade our injured ones as mental cases. We revered them as Oldtime Americans revered their soldier casualties, knowing they

[98]

gave in greater measure with greater bravery and more risk to themselves. We protected, loved, and encouraged our injured ones, knowing that in them the will to fight and the will to love were striving most mightily for expression and that they had been singled out for attack in a world that was afraid of these very qualities.

We seldom lost a Human Being to Human Anguish, as long as we got to her before the psychiatrists did; and we grew in numbers and in reputation among uncommitted women. Had we been able to win over men to the cause of Liberty and Love, we would have grown still more, reproducing and filling the land with Human Beings.

Instead our end came with a swiftness and finality unparalleled in American history, even by the repression of the American Indian, the American Jew, the American Black, and the Conquered Peoples of the World. Male America had been driven into an increasingly defensive position, first by the assaults of the Furies, then by the temptations of the Sweethearts, and finally by this awesome offer of Liberty and Love from the Human Beings. Increasingly men had begun to band together and to declare their activities off limits to Women. The final tragedy began on such an occasion, a Males' Day football game.

It was half time in the Los Angeles Coliseum in a championship game between the Seattle Satyrs and the San Francisco Chauvinists. As part of the half-time festivities, the Astronaut of the Year Award was being given to Jack Armstrong, a Tenth-generation Armstrong Astronaut. This year's award was particularly momentous, for America's most distant intergalactic probe was thought to have encountered definite but unfathomable communications from another form of life in outer space. Everyone anticipated that Armstrong would make significant remarks in regard to these new findings.

Armstrong was introduced to the stadium fans and to the millions of Q Tube viewers by the half-time M.C., and he immediately declared that every American Astronaut was prepared to fight to his death to defend our liberty from this as yet unidentified form of life in outer space.

In the midst of this speech, the M.C. stepped forward, threw off his clothes and displayed himself as an unmistakable female. Seizing the microphone from the stunned Armstrong, she declared:

"Give Life a chance! Liberty and Love make Life! Let us protect ourselves, yes! But let us offer love to every living creature, Human Beings and all others!"

Armstrong recovered his composure, put his arm around the half-nude Human Being, called her "Sweet-tart," and offered her "a little love," amid hilarious applause from a hundred thousand men and untold millions of male viewers. The Human Being grabbed his arm and tossed him to the ground. She began to speak again to the hushed audience, but in an instant Armstrong had leaped upon her. Avoiding his grasp, she struck him to the ground with a karate chop.

She was seized, and a frenzied mob began tearing the stadium apart. Broken goalposts, wooden bleachers, team benches, billboards, fences, newspapers, game programs, TV and movie film strips, plastic drink containers, clothing, even hot dogs and hamburgers were piled up to make an enormous pyre in the middle of the field. The Human Being was tied to a broken goalpost and staked out on top. Then the whole thing was set ablaze.

As the Human Being went up in flames, her voice sang out

> Praise Life
> Life is One
> Praise the One
> Who shares the Life.
>
> Life is One!
> One Life!

[100]

She died with the words "One Life!" ringing through the stadium and across the nation.

The following day brought an unparalleled response of remorse and shame throughout Male America. A woman burned to death! While millions of men stood by! A young woman, as it turned out, hardly more than a girl!

Throughout the nation gallant men banded together to protect their women from a repetition of this martyrdom. Furies, Sweethearts, and Human Beings alike were rounded up and placed in protective detention, not to be released again except in the custody of a male. Overnight, the Women's Movement came to an end in America. Overnight, every Human Being in America had been locked up or forced into hiding.

9th Entry

When everyone at our Pleasure Party was already high on two- and three-LSD Equivalents of Punch, a young Good Lay in the corner began hallucinating into the blank Q Tube, and I resolved to take no more than One Quarter dose.

A Dynamo by the girl's side was attempting to calm her. "Try Free-Associating," he urged.

"Cunt," the girl said. "I am a cunt, cunt, cunt, cunt, cunt, cunt, cunt..."

"No, Free-Associate."

"I am!" she screamed at him. "I *am* a cunt, cunt, cunt..."

My Girl gave her an antipsychotic injection, and within seconds she was sitting becalmed on the floor.

In a corner, three or four Dynamos were sitting in a tangle of wires trying to hook up their Pleasure Pack energizers in parallel, one to another, for a super dose of pleasure to the last Dynamo in line.

A Bureaucrat slapped me on the thigh and gestured toward the group tangled in its own wires.

[103]

"I'll take a good Cocksucker to a Pleasure Pack in Parallel anytime." He laughed.

"Bag Off," I told him. I was feeling dangerously Oversensitive.

My Girl was in another corner, learning to play the electronic computer with a fellow Bureaucrat from NAMS, My Old Buddy, no less. They were Taking some Pleasure in each other's bodies, as is the custom at our parties; little feels and pokes and titillations.

My Secretary sidled up to me. "Do you see what Your Old Buddy is doing with Your Girl?"

Before I met Gambol, I had Bagged my Secretary a few times, like any Dynamic Boss.

My Old Buddy left My Girl and came over to me.

"Buddy Check!" He winked and grinned at me.

"Buddy Check yourself," I said. I didn't have to Take Him Seriously at a party. At work, I'd have to start confiding in him, a sort of casual Attitude Check.

"Just Keeping Tabs on Your Girl," he said and headed back to her.

I took another drink. Still, I was unaffected—Rogar, the man with an ego as strong as Theron. He never Blows His Mind.

My heart was beating very strongly, and I must have looked a bit pale, for My Girl came across the room and asked me, "Are you feeling all right, My Man? I don't see you Taking any Pleasure. Are you jealous of me and Your Old Buddy?"

"No, My Girl, enjoy yourself."

She gave my navel a friendly thrust with her finger,

[104]

then bounced back to her Dynamo and his music machine.

I put my hand upon my heart, and then, unexpectedly—

Thump! My heart whacked the inside of my chest.

Thump! Again, and then it stood still!

And then—

SWACK! An enormous blow from within! Followed by dead silence, a still heart.

I will collapse!

WHACK! and I am brought back to life again.

And now I can look down at my naked chest.

There is a shadow across it, the dark round shadow cast by our Bubble as we fled the death on the mountain.

No, a gaping hole.

And within that hole I see my heart, quivering but not beating.

What a marvelous trip! Now my chest a cage of flesh and muscle and bone with my heart beating out an empty space; now my bones beaten away, just muscle and skin clinging to my sides; and now I am a gutted carcass, disemboweled, empty of all my insides except my heart, my heart in a great hollow made of nothing but skin; I am a thick skin drying in the sun, pounded clean and dry from within; and now my dry skin is disappearing, smashed to smithereens.

I leap up and scream. "I need her!" I am trembling all over, white and shaking, and My Girl is beside me now, easing me down upon the couch.

[105]

I hear the whispers, "Rogar, of all people, Rogar, having such a bad trip. Such a bad trip."

"Take his hand."

"Pet his head."

"Give him a Grouper Hug."

"Don't talk, My Man. Don't talk. It's all right," My Girl tells me. "I'm Your Dependent, Rogar, and you're Mine."

"My Dependent," I murmur, while others reassure me: "It's all right, Rogar, we're with you . . . We'll take care of you . . . It's just a bad trip."

My Girl smiles. "You're My Dependent, and I love you. I love you even *without* an Official Contract of Mutual Emotional Dependency."

"I was drinking Punch, wasn't I?"

"Yes, My Dependent, yes. You've had a very bad trip if you can't even remember that."

"Very bad," I murmur.

"It's beautiful holding your hand like this, My Man. It's the most wonderful Mutual Emotional Dependency we've ever shared. I feel ready for an Official Contract."

And then she leans over to suck my cock. A grown Good Lay, My Girl; she is sucking my cock like a little Cocksucker—in public, letting all the world know she gives herself to me in utter Dependency.

As I begin coming into her mouth, she pulls my pike away from her and sprays my fluids against the wall. I watch my stuff slide downward.

And here, at my own Pleasure Party, I am overwhelmed with trembling and can barely hold back my bladder and bowels—the worst attack of GUILT, SHAME, and ANXIETY that I have ever known.

"What a Dynamo you are," My Girl says. "You're just dying to Bag me!"

She takes me by the hand and leads me upstairs to our Love Room. The Bag is in the corner near a couch.

"My Girl, I'm sorry, but I don't want to go Into the Bag with you."

She stares at me. "You've had a bad trip, that's all."

"No. My Girl, I've got to tell you. Our Mutual Emotional Dependency is coming to an end."

"There's another woman! Your Secretary?"

I shake my head.

"My Man, listen to me, I don't care if you're Bagging another Lay. Maybe your Ego needs it. You could even bring her to one of our parties. We could get some New Fixtures and go into a Triple Bag together!"

I should do something to smooth away the wrinkles in her brow.

"My Man, I know I didn't suck well tonight, I know I still have Hangups. But I'll swallow it next time, I will!"

I try to say it as gently as I can. "I don't want you to suck."

"But you used to beg me."

"I've changed."

"*You've* changed? Look what you're doing to *me.*"

"Your pain is your own. Our bodies aren't connected."

As I spoke, hearing Gambol's voice within me, I was

startled by a sharp slap across my face. Then My Girl was upon me, her nails going at my face.

I restrained her. Afterward, she sobbed and apologized, and I had all I could do to keep up my resolve to terminate our Dependency.

Perhaps it is written somewhere that a man must suffer before he can leave his Dependents.

Written somewhere?

It is carved deep within my CHILDHOOD.

10th Entry

Gambol has not called me in ten days, but I have respected her wish not to see or hear from me. I have read and reread the history of the Human Beings she gave me, and it has encouraged me to complete my own history of the People. So my work remains my salvation, though I now know it is not enough for happiness.

I continue to study the history of the Human Beings, but I cannot seem to do what she expected of me—to apply it to our relationship and to myself. I cannot believe that I have anything in common with those Leftover Male Americans who made a martyr of the Human Being.

I seem to lack that same understanding of my own histories. I read—as you will read—what I have learned about Jew Pricing. But I cannot apply it to myself.

A HISTORY OF THE PEOPLE

Until relatively modern times, the People were of so little interest to anyone that historians virtually ignored them. Some historians have gone so far as to say that the People were the invention of the Jewish Prophet Karl Marx, who identified them as the workers, the Group allegedly exploited by an elite capitalist class holding ownership of the means of production. Marx prophesied that this capitalist system would eventually generate enormous industrial monopolies, ever greater unemployment and exploitation, and an eventual revolution by the People.

By the mid-Twentieth Century a few dozen families did own or control most of the country, and by the Twenty-first Century the nation's industry was merged into one giant monolith, United American Goodwill Industries, Inc. The People one and all became Goodwill Workers. The prophecy of increased unemployment and exploitation was also fulfilled, and most of the People became idle or employed at worthless, demeaning tasks. But by the last quarter of the century, it was already apparent that the Marxist prediction of a revolution would be foiled by a spectacular innovation: the government would *pay* the People to remain idle and worthless. Thus the capitalist elite continued to own the means of production, while the government elite used the Guaranteed Income to buy and own the People. The People, of course, continued to own nothing.

This invigorating competition between the People Owners and the Industry Owners led to continued economic growth in America, limited only by the dwindling of our natural resources and the burden of reimbursing the People for their worthlessness. The People themselves were lulled into contentment by the Media, who continually reminded them that, idle and worthless though they were, they were still the best-paid People in the world.

Russia, America's chief rival, had made the fatal mistake of permitting the Government to own *both* the means of production and the People, thus eliminating all internal competition. The Russian economy began to decline, and it at last became apparent why she had so busily hoarded her Jews since the Twentieth Century.

[110]

By threatening her Jewish population with extinction, and forcing Israel to buy back its Jews, Russia was able to supplement her depleted treasury. Thus the expression "selling your Jews" came to indicate a last-ditch attempt at solvency, comparable to but more creative than "scraping the bottom of the barrel."

Russia's financial coup was made possible by the Jews of America, whose solicitude for their People made them willing to pay the ransom. This generosity of course carried the stipulation that the Russian Jews be prevented from emigrating to America itself, where everyone, American Jews included, felt that the Jewish population was more than large enough.

It is generally agreed that without this buying and selling of Jews to bring capital into Russia from America, the floor of the international money market would have fallen out completely. As it was, the individual Jew replaced the abandoned Gold Standard in backing the world's currencies. Nonetheless, the Jew himself became a target of increasing hatred as the People of the world realized that they couldn't earn a Jew Price for themselves with a lifetime of labor, even if they sold themselves into economic slavery.

The nations of the world—never enthusiastic about saving Jews—now demanded that Israel permit multilateral control of the flow of Jews in order to maintain the stability of the International Jew Price. But while American Jews had a virtually limitless capacity to pay, buying Jews from Russia soon reached the point of diminishing returns for Israel, since every Jew bought made more money available to Russia for military aid to the Arabs. Declaring, "A Jew bought costs a Jew killed," Israel abruptly suspended the Law of Return which since 1951 had guaranteed every Jew in the world the right to come to Israel as a citizen. Overnight the Jew Price plummeted as frantic international speculators tried to sell each other Jews when no one wanted them any more. Even the most heinous atrocities against Jews around the world could not induce Israel to resume the ransoming; and American Jewry, still willing to pay anything, balked at persuading its own government to admit any Jews to America. All around the world stronger nations tried to force weaker nations to buy Jews from them, but to no avail.

Once the Jew Price hit zero, Russia's shaky economy collapsed, followed quickly by economic disaster for the other major Jew Hoarders, including the Arab nations, the United German Republic, and England. These nations even resorted to offering their own People on the international market, each touting its own particular virtues: the Arabs their ingratiating docility, the Germans their dogged persistence, the English their sense of decency. But because this smacked of outright slavery, or more likely because there had always been a glut of ordinary People on the market, these efforts failed. Of all the People of the world, only the Jewish People would pay a cent to ransom their own. This situation resulted in another round of vicious persecutions against the Jews.

China and its allies alone were untouched by this international economic crisis. China had always refused to buy and sell Jews, partly on the principle that it was a capitalist perversion, and partly because she had harbored a deep-seated aversion to any dealings with Jews ever since the series of betrayals by the Lessinger-led American governments.

When China successfully moved in the United Nations to replace a moribund Russia with her own ally, the People's Republic of Albania, an embittered Russia began breaking all her international ties, even to the Arabs. But Arabs do not give up so easily as Russians. Backed by world opinion, which blamed the Jews for the economic chaos in the world, and still armed with Soviet weapons, the Arabs spilled over the Israeli borders in what they billed as the One-day Offensive.

The offensive lasted only thirty seconds, the approximate time it took Israel to set off the atomic land mines that rimmed its borders. When the rising heaps of

[112]

sand settled to earth again, Israel and the Sinai had become a plateau standing in the midst of a moat, and the Suez Canal had been plowed open for the first time in centuries. The surviving civilian populations on both sides could do little more than gape at each other across mile-deep trenches.

This thirty-second war was given a special name by the American People, whose favorite Prime Time TV programs were interrupted by a Special Bulletin reporting the Arab offensive. Mercifully the war was so short that the Bulletin announcing its onset lasted long enough to announce its conclusion as well, and a grateful viewing public nicknamed it "The Spot Commercial War."

A traditionally anti-Semitic United Nations retaliated by assigning Israel the Arab Mandate—responsibility for taking care of the demoralized peoples of the Middle East. Israel accepted and soon published a White Paper invoking certain unsavory racial qualities of non-Jewish Semitic Peoples to justify Arab subjugation to Israel.

The poor Hebrews, harassed, hounded, and persecuted by all the world for four thousand years, thus found themselves overwhelmed with responsibilities for others less fortunate than themselves. Even a world rife with anti-Semitism was forced to admit that the customary Jewish qualities of humanism, tolerance, and decency had been undermined by these unprecedented responsibilities. As an expression to describe an ultimate perversion of moral character, it became customary in U.N. circles to speak of "a Jew with an Arab on his back."

This moral vacuum was filled by Communist China, who had been inexorably pursuing that policy once characterized so eloquently by Chairman Mao as "ownership of the People by the People and for the People." By the year 2100 the Chinese had proceeded so far that the People would soon own everything without anyone owning the People.

The American Media found itself increasingly unable to ignore China's stupendous achievements. Even *Time* magazine was forced to comment, "The Chinese People may be better off than we are, but at least we don't have to read Mao's poetry." A disgruntled American People now arose as one to demand that they be paid still more for remaining idle and worthless.

Worldwide fear of the Chinese Menace now enabled the United States to plot a global offensive against the People of the World under the guise of an allied attack on China. In one grand stroke—whose details I hope yet to uncover—we wiped out our allies and enemies alike. Ownership of *all* the world's industry fell into the hands of United American Goodwill Industries, Inc., while ownership of *all* the world's Peoples fell into the hands of the United States Government. Thus did the Good War fulfill the aims of three centuries of American Foreign Policy.

In the long-standing tradition of the two-party system, the Industry Owners renamed themselves the Republican Party of the World and the People Owners renamed themselves the Democratic Party of the World. Henceforth, election campaigns between the two were promoted as World Championships. The People, of course, paid to be spectators at these Party Games.

Minor political readjustments were required to keep up with these more precise definitions of ownership. Many of the nation's labor leaders, for example, attempted to place themselves squarely among the Republican Industrial Elite with the claim, "People, too, are Raw Materials."

There was never any doubt that the Military should abandon its Government ties and cast its lot with United American Goodwill Industries, Inc. Nearly every retired Military Officer of any rank was already in the employ of Industry, and, as had been long understood, even those in Preretirement Uniform were responsible directly to the Industrialists. It was therefore only natural that the Military should leave the Government and

[114]

incorporate as Investors United for Defense (IUD), the largest and most active subsidiary of United American Goodwill Industries, Inc. From then on, whenever the People of the Conquered Lands resisted development by United American Goodwill Industries, Inc., it became a simple matter to order War Games to be played in their area. These Games were so effective in reducing any foreign nation to a heap of decomposing organic matter that the Military coined a phrase for it—"Recycling our enemies."

Meanwhile less and less was heard from the American People. Those few uprisings that did break out inevitably centered around demands for better home Q-tube programing. Then, with the development of Capping, even the most idle and worthless worker could be entertained to the very core of his brain. To this day, the greater part of the American public spend most of their day bobbing beneath their Caps.

Now that nearly everyone seems to be a Bureaucrat, no one is even sure how many People still remain. Comparatively speaking, there may be very few left in America. They seem to live well enough on the outskirts of the suburbs in fine Highrises with gardens, pools, and sports arenas. But to tell the truth, a Bureaucrat like myself can go through the entire year without meeting a single one of them.

11th Entry

I inserted my Mental Health Credit Card and watched
the Security Monitor flash "Sound Mind, Sound
Credit." Then I stepped into the great domed room and
stood amid lurid lights, rising aphrodisiac scents, gyrating shapes upon the ceiling and the walls, and electronic
orgasms popping through the sound system. The dome
itself was an enormous inverted screen, beneath which I
would become one small orgasm tuning up to the great
environmental Coming. But even the breathing of the
diaphragmatic floor beneath my naked feet failed to
Turn Me On.

A young Lay with rich red hair, frail shoulders, and
full swollen breasts approached me.

Spindly and anemic compared to Gambol.

"Feeling any Pain?" she asked.

"No, not much of anything."

She handed me a drink laced with a mild halluci-
nogen and led me to one of the Pleasure Cubicles that
rimmed the Dome.

"What would you like to feel? What's Your Thing today?"

Obliviation is what I want. Gone is my Great Book resolve.

"I don't really know," I said as I sat down cross-legged with her in the cubicle and stared at all the dials on the Pleasure Panel: sound, scent, vibration, even a special Pleasure Pack hookup.

"Don't Know Your Thing?" She giggled. "Poor mixed-up Dynamo. You need a good Bagging."

"What would *you* like to feel?" I asked her.

"Me? Oh, I feel whatever the man wants, and you can be sure that means I feel everything before the day is over. This is *your* hour!"

She stretched me out upon the pulsating foam floor and began brushing my face with her breasts.

"Do you like my nipples?" she asked.

They looked glazed, like candy apples. "Cherry is a good flavor," I said.

"It's natural, too."

"Have you ever let a man near your naked cunt?"

"That's *not* natural," she said. "Go Bag Yourself!"

"Only kidding," I told her.

She was making tender expressions, sweetly massaging me all over my face, touching my aching lids and my tense facial muscles, stroking under my arms.

"Good hands."

"Nice pike."

Gambol, with her head bent over my lap . . .

I lost my erection.

[118]

"You're not an *Official,* are you?" she asked.

"No, just a plain old Bureaucrat."

"Then why'd you ask me about naked cunts? Are you conducting some kind of Quality Control Test? No one has ever lost an erection over me."

"I was making a joke. Turn the music and the vibes up a little more, and I'll roll right into the Bag with you."

She adjusted two dials and came back, all set to share pleasure.

We put the Bag between us, and she inflated it slowly, not with the usual Porto-bag gas but with the special hydraulic fluids used in Pleasure Domes. The Bag swelled until I could no longer reach my arms around it; then I slipped myself into the cock slot. Inside, it was warm and well lubricated, and my pike grew. As she manipulated and hugged the Bag and urged me closer into it, the hydraulic pressures enveloped and squeezed my pike with a firmness and a sensuality that the best-trained Cocksucker could never imitate. Then, as the Bag swelled still larger, she inserted the Hydraulic Plastic Penis into her cunt; and with each thrust of my pike into the Bag's Hydraulic Cunt, the great responsive Plastic Penis on her end swelled and thrust into her with a strength and power to shame the Cock of the most manly Dynamo. Meeting each returning hydraulic cunt spasm, my cock grew still larger.

She manipulated the Bag with all the skill of her training—her fingers, hands, arms squeezing titillating sensations through the fluids within it.

[119]

"There, there," she reassured me. "Now you're feeling better. There, feel the Bag between us."

As she churned her breasts against her side of the Bag, I could feel the spongy cushions of flesh sending great pulses through to me. My pelvis began thrusting my pike into the Bag; and I could see the surprise, even the shock upon her face—for I was thrusting wildly, driving the hydraulic penis into her, into her, into her, into her, into her screaming, thrusting, buttocks-blazing, Bag-exploding, rubber-foaming Obliviating Frantasy.

"NOW!" she breathed over and over again as she lay unmoving and exhausted beneath the dead Bag. "NOW!"

"Now," I repeated mournfully.

12th Entry

Every Attitude Check has become a life-or-death trial. I'm afraid the most routine examination of my Free Associations may reveal me as I am.

As I am? The phrase plumbs the depths of my Great Book Hallucination. But I've lost my Visions as I've gained the fearful symptoms. And they grow worse.

My joints are beginning to ache again, a flu-like sensation complete with feverishness, heaviness in the head, a thickening within the chest. But at least I've stopped missing Gambol so much.

I have found a document which purports to explain everything about the Hebrew Disease, but I don't know what to make of it. It could even be material planted to attract traitors and dissenters for easy identification. Or is this paranoia on my part, another symptom of the Disease itself?

The film carries an Official stamp, indicating some degree of censorship. But perhaps it adhered too closely to the truth and offered too much information to be published as Official History.

[121]

THIRTY-FIVE HUNDRED YEARS
OF THE
HEBREW DISEASE

In the year 3500 Before the Good War, Egypt was beset by periodic plagues culminating in one devastating epidemic which struck down all the first-born sons throughout the land. When the Pharaoh discovered that only the children of the Jews had been spared, he was wise enough to realize what this meant—that the Jews carried the Disease while remaining immune to its worst effects—and he resolved to drive the mass of infected people into the Red Sea. But pity beclouded this great king's judgment, and he permitted the last survivors to escape across the water. Hence the expression "to pity a Jew" describes the ultimate in tragically misguided sympathy for the underdog.

Thrown together with their own infected tribesmen, isolated from all healthy influences in the wastelands of the Sinai, exhausted and yet grateful for a lease on their miserable lives—the Jews began to worship the imagined Source of their Affliction. If they could live with their Disease, their Prophet Moses promised them, then their Disease would wipe out all their enemies. "Worship God and keep his Disease," became their Commandment; and so wholeheartedly did they embrace this teaching that they kept a record of IT in an endless, confused Journal marked by that Hebraic combination of GUILT, SHAME, and ANXIETY, buttressed with PRIDE. This scroungy band of pestilent nomads scourged the Sinai and finally descended upon the hapless land of Canaan.

No doubt the Disease would have continued to gain in virulence until it destroyed the Jews themselves, thus ending their threat to mankind, had not the Assyrians, the Babylonians, and then the Romans tried to treat the Contagion by dispersing the Jews through the civilized world. The Roman Diaspora spread IT to the benign-looking Gentiles of the Empire, and for the first time, apparently innocuous non-Jews became carriers. Hence the expression a "Roman Solution"—in contrast to a "Final Solution"—has come to mean any halfway measure that merely disguises the severity of the problem.

The tragic consequences of this dispersion of the Jews can best be understood statistically, for their total numbers may have exceeded eight million, ten percent or more of the population of the Roman Empire. Since most were forced to settle within sparsely populated European lands that later became great nations, it must be frankly admitted that almost every living person in the Western World suffers from a genetic Jewish taint.

The new Gentile victims of this weaker Strain of GUILT, SHAME, and ANXIETY were called Christians, ironically named for the most innocuous Jewish Prophet, and the Strain itself became known as Christianity, or C-Strain.

Long before modern psychosomatic medicine, the people of the Middle Ages realized the connection between the Jews and the plagues, and tens of thousands of Jews were periodically slaughtered or driven from their homes. Yet these same Christians preserved the evil Journal of the Jews—all the while slaughtering the Jewish people without mercy. "Killing the Authors but keeping the Book" thus describes hopelessly misguided attempts at religious, moral, and political reform.

Toward the end of the Middle Ages, C-Strain further deteriorated into numerous competing Mutants. For some reason, C-Strain victims can never appreciate the deadly nature of their own Infection—and yet are readily able to see its bad effects in anyone suffering from the slightest variation of it. Thus, for a hundred years, C-Strain Mutants periodically killed each other off with an enthusiasm they usually reserved for Jews.

Meanwhile, C-Strain was inbred feverishly among monks behind cloistered walls, then spread outside those walls by Missionary Carriers. America's indigenous

Indian population was nearly killed off to the last man by this particular Mutant, and an imported Negro population was purposely infected to weaken the slaves and assure their subjugation to their already debilitated C-Strain masters.

Despite these beginnings, IT rapidly declined in America. The country was too thinly populated and too individualistic to support a contagious social disease. By the Twentieth Century, the Plague of the Ages had the status of the Common Cold in America—everyone expected an occasional mild infection.

Then the unexpected happened. With the Hebrew Disease no longer an apparent threat in America or Europe, the largest onslaught of all time was launched against IT. Striving to avoid the catastrophic "Roman Solution" of the Diaspora, the Nazi Germans directed their efforts against the entire Jewish People, and in less than a decade, their "Final Solution" had nearly eradicated IT from the face of Europe. One third of all Jews in the world were dead.

Examined NOW from the perspective of several centuries, this Nazi purge of the Hebrews can be appreciated for what it was. The Germans, after all, might well have won World War II had they made use of their Jews, as America used Einstein, and avoided the expense of eliminating them. Hence the expression "Nazi" NOW denotes anyone who unselfishly sacrifices everything in the pursuit of his ideals.

Even the most bitter rivals of the Nazis—Russia, England, and the United States—helped make this Solution a Final one. Stalin, Churchill, and Roosevelt each distinguished himself by refusing to publicize its magnitude, by refusing to threaten retaliation as they had on the occasion of other "atrocities," and, most important, by refusing to allow Hebrews sanctuary in any other land while they still had a chance to flee Europe. During the war Russians manned some of the worst extermination camps and participated in mass murders such as Babi Yar. Great Britain diverted her

[124]

precious military resources to make sure that no Jews escaped from Europe to Palestine, where she was protecting the interests of the pro-Nazi Arabs. The President of the United States and the Congress both turned their backs on a boatload of refugee Jews waiting offshore near Miami, forcing the ship to return its entire cargo to the extermination camps of Nazi Germany. Specific plans for immobilizing the death-camp trains were rejected by the allied military, and not a single crematorium was damaged by direct attack. Hitler himself waited for tacit approval from the Allies before implementing the Final Solution, for he feared the effects of a united world opinion. Hence the Final Solution goes down in history as the first concerted effort of the nations of the world to clean up their environment.

But this massive public health effort backfired by causing an intensification of GUILT, SHAME, and ANXIETY in the surviving Jewish population of the world. These "Reactivated Hebrews" managed to spread so much GUILT, SHAME, and ANXIETY to the Gentile world that the Gentiles grudgingly allowed them to return to their apparently worthless "homeland" in Palestine, leaving the unfortunate indigenous Arabs to bear the furious brunt of THAT which had survived the onslaught of the most advanced nations of the world for 3500 years. "To kill a Jew" thus expresses mankind's chronic frustration in the control and elimination of its most dreadful problems.

Ultimately it fell to America to find the Cure. In cases of cancer, it is sometimes necessary to subject the entire body to massive doses of atomic radiation, nearly killing the body to kill the tumor. So it came to pass in the Good War that America treated the world with global radiation to save it from Israel and the Hebrew Disease.

But the Hebrew Disease seems to thrive on adversity, and it flared up more intensely than ever after Our Great Victory. Our President, aware that even the

[125]

Emperor Constantine had succumbed to the Infection, placed himself in solitary confinement, venturing abroad from Pentagon Towers only within the isolation of the Presidential Bubble, whose seams cannot be breached by the smallest particle of GUILT, SHAME, or ANXIETY.

Our scientific Bureaucracy meanwhile concentrated its resources on the attempt to isolate the causative agent—the GUILT, SHAME, and ANXIETY Factor, a presumed subviral antilife substance known among biochemists as the "elusive GSA Particle". The Media helped by giving enthusiastic publicity to any scientist with a claim that this or that Particle in the blood or urine was the cause of GUILT, SHAME, and ANXIETY in one of its many manifestations—schizophrenia, depression, alcoholism, drug addiction, criminality, aggressiveness, passivity, impotence, frigidity, stupidity, homosexuality, alienation, adolescence, illiteracy, and poverty.

But even the most painstaking analysis of liters and liters of Jewish Tears could not separate out the elusive GSA factor.

Despairing of an answer from the Physical Scientists, a weary and frustrated President took it upon himself to ask the Social Scientists the one question that had stymied them: "Why the fuck are you afraid of Oversimplifying?"

"*I've* never been afraid of Simplifying!" cried a single voice from among all the Bureaucratic Scientists, and B. S. Fakir rose, brandishing his famous book, *Beyond People,* as evidence. He had already shown his ability to oversimplify the behavior of the mouse and the rat; it was a still easier feat to oversimplify the life of a man. His theory—"Of molecules, mice, and men"— proved there were no differences between the oscillations of an atom, the appetites of a rodent, and the spiritual needs of a human being. Revered among his colleagues, royally supported by grants from the National Institute for Mental Health, and already rewarded with a Best Seller, this scientific paragon of

[126]

Simple-minded Dependency assumed leadership of the President's Commission for Mental Security.

In one stroke, the Commission created a new concept to bridge the differences between the Social Science theory and the Police practices, and the Simplification was born. And in another stroke, the Commission proposed what would become the nation's greatest Bureaucracy, the National Agency for Mental Security (NAMS)—that perfect combination of Social Science and Security Police—to make up Simplifications and to implement them.

Why *had* the Social Sciences been afraid of Oversimplifying? Because the Jews, led by Marx and Freud, had confounded that purity and simplicity which had always characterized Gentile thought. Freud was probably the most dangerous Carrier since Moses—the sickest Jew of all, he valued solitude and work at the expense of pleasure and good fellowship. Freud wanted to liberate his client from his past without making him *Dependent* upon anyone! Luckily, few of Freud's disciples took seriously his injunctions to avoid Oversimplifying and Dependency. Most of them wanted to control their clients as much as any Security Officer, and by the 1970s, the average Jewish practitioner was as Simpleminded as any Gentile.

Marx, while turning against his Hebrew Heritage and displaying tendencies toward Simplification and Dependency, still had remained implacably committed to an ideal of truth that defied Simplification. In his personal life he was as great a loner as Freud, and his collectivism was inspired by a Jewish devotion to individual fulfillment—always the eternal enemy of Group Dependency. By the 1970s, however, American Marxism had degenerated to Liberalism, except for a few diehard Radicals, whose sloganeering was itself a forerunner of Simplification.

By the time of the President's Commission, no Jewish loner was alive to threaten the Commission's unanimous endorsement of the Simplification, and the

[127]

average American's longing for Simpleminded Dependency could no longer be denied.

It fell to our President to announce the first Simplifications to the nation.

In homes all over the stricken land, the Guilty, the Ashamed, and the Anxious gathered before their Q Tubes. The unkept promises of two centuries of Presidents and two thousand years of Messiahs were about to be fulfilled in two great simplifications that would cure the nation and save the people from their GUILT, SHAME, and ANXIETY!

Our President began by recalling how America's greatness had been realized by the Winning of the Good War with hardly a casualty. Those millions of our forces stationed abroad with their families, our diplomatic corps, advisers and consultants, the several million tourists and businessmen abroad celebrating the Year 2100—these token sacrifices were more than justified by the utter righteousness of our actions. No nation, our President made clear, had ever before reigned supreme over the entire earth, because no nation had dared to act with such unflinching devotion to its own righteousness.

Having clarified and distilled our righteousness, the President now triumphantly announced that one unfailing American Truth, that great and still greatest of all our Simplifications:

MIGHT MAKES RIGHT
and
RIGHT MAKES MIGHT

Barely were the words spoken when the Billboard behind the President bleeped and flashed Galloping Feedback from the entire nation. With lights and buzzers and sirens going off behind him like a Fourth of July display, he raised both his arms over his head and shouted: "I banish GUILT, SHAME, and ANXIETY from our land! I pronounce the end of doubt and ambivalence about ourselves! I free each citizen to feel GOOD FEELINGS for NOW and for ALL TIME!"

As the marquee of the Billboard itself lit up with the words of the first Simplification, the nation swelled with a tidal wave of GOOD FEELINGS, rising higher and higher upon the crest of that great couplet, that Simplification so perfect that it came out equally true when the Billboard flashed it upside down:

RIGHT MAKES MIGHT

and

MIGHT MAKES RIGHT

The President raised his arms again, his armpit seams splitting with his exuberant gesture, and, when the Billboard and America were again quiet, he announced his second great Simplification, thereby projecting the nation into an orbit of dizzy GOOD FEELING and WELL-BEING, a consummate state of SIMPLEMINDED DEPENDENCY never before achieved by any nation upon Earth:

GOOD PEOPLE ARE WINNERS

and

WINNERS FEEL GOOD

13th Entry

"You're Playing Games with us," a Grouper complained in my direction. "You haven't been here in weeks, and now you won't *share* anything with us."

I should have gone to Group elsewhere. It's one of the great American freedoms: the right to Group in the Egg of your choice. The Egg has replaced the Oldtime Church as the architectural symbol and bulwark of the nation's religious life; any NOW American can travel across the country "Egg-safe" in the knowledge that in his time of need he can always find an Egg to crawl into.

Our Grouper Egg is perched upon the roof of my office wing here at NAMS. The ledges and roofs around the entire building are festooned with other Office Eggs, so that the building, like many others around the city, looks like a giant cubist bird's nest bristling with enormous eggs.

Newer ones like ours are made of Theron, and stand on a narrow pedestal. This creates the astonishing impression that the American landscape has been bombed by monster chickens dropping thirty-foot eggs.

[131]

Grouper Leader was sitting beside the Pleasure Panel, whose neon message sign blinked the First Commandment: "What's Good for the Group is Good for You."

"You look all Pent Up." My Buddy kept the attention on me. "Nobody wants to Pit you," he reassured me.

I hope not.

I glanced around at the familiar faces: My Girl, My Old Buddy, My Secretary, Grouper Leader, some of the office Dynamos and Their Girls, and half a dozen people I couldn't place at all, including an attractive blond Good Lay.

"We *missed* you," said the blond Lay.

"We *need* you," said someone else.

"You really want help, or you wouldn't make yourself the Center of Attention."

"But I haven't *said* anything to make myself the Center of Attention."

"That's just it!" said Grouper Leader.

If I'm not careful, they will Yolk me, Scoop me, and Pit me!

"Are you having DOUBTS?" Grouper Leader asked me.

A hush.

"Do any one of you feel Egg-safe all the time?" I said. "Are you always certain that What's Good for the Group is Good for You?"

"The Group—love it or leave it!" an older man cried out.

That's a new one.

[132]

Blond Good Lay got up and sat next to me. As she began stroking me with warm, light fingers and gentle palm pressures, I recognized the touch of a Professional Playgirl.

It is not the hand of Gambol.

"I need eye contact with you," said Playgirl.

Pale-blue eyes, limpid eyes, yearning eyes. Her emptiness called to me, and I felt a stirring in my Ball Pack.

"Dynamo, it's all right." Playgirl touched my shoulder and drew me closer beside her. "Here." She offered her nipple, small and pink.

Even My Girl was nodding—anything to get me to act Dependently.

I shook my head.

"Afraid to be an Anxious Adult like the rest of us!" someone accused me.

"You think you're Special!"

"You think you can Judge everyone else."

"What's Good for US is Good for YOU!"

Each ejaculation was accompanied by discordant stabs of organ music, and the Yolk of the Egg—the scoop at the bottom of the shell—glowed a murky yellow, as if the Egg Yolk had settled to the bottom.

Playgirl draped her arm over my shoulder, urging me to join her in the Pit.

"You seem so in touch with his deeper feelings," Grouper Leader told Playgirl. "*You* should play his Alter Ego." He turned to My Old Buddy. "And you'll be THE GROUP."

My Old Buddy slid down the contour to wait for me

[133]

in the bottom of the shell, eager to speak to me for THE GROUP.

With Playgirl's arm around my waist, we glided down into the Pit and came to a rest. Now My Alter Ego, she pressed against my back, while My Buddy, as THE GROUP, faced me knee to knee. He was Revving Up with serious rapidly flexed Facial Expressions to show his interest in the encounter.

My Buddy began with the traditional GROUP opener. "We all want to help you."

"With what?" I asked.

"With whatever you *need.*"

"You're Egging Me On," I said. "Trying to Scoop me."

"Only for your own good," said THE GROUP.

My Alter Ego spoke in her sweet voice for my real feelings. "I try to act like a tough Dynamo, but I feel defensive and easily hurt today."

"No," I said, breaking the rules, contradicting my Alter Ego. "That's not what I meant at all."

"You do sound defensive," said THE GROUP.

"I'm afraid you'll reject me," My Alter Ego explained for me. "I feel left out, small, and frightened. I don't even Know My Own Thing any more."

"Bag Off!" I broke in on them. "I've been experiencing myself! Do any of you know what that *really* means?"

"I feel so alone," my Alter Ego persisted. "And I'm afraid no one will understand and love me." I felt her breasts swelling against my shoulders with each soft whisper.

[134]

My Girl came sliding down on top of us within the Pit. Playgirl and My Buddy welcomed her with great Grouper Hugs, reaching around me for each other as if I were some sort of obstacle in their midst.

As My Buddy tried to get a feel of Playgirl and My Girl at the same time—let him have them!—My Secretary came piling onto us.

There were others all over me now—hands and fingers reassuring me, feeling me, loving and feeling and reassuring each other—the bottom of the PIT as alive as a can of worms.

Grouper Leader, the only one left Up Against the Wall, filled the room with romantic music, warm air, and a lovely orange-blossom scent.

Gambol! I called silently from beneath the heap of smothering bodies.

Gradually the movements were slowing down. Two Groupers held hands at my crotch, moaning "Wow" and "Now"; another's face was being forced against my belly. I gasped for breath between a pair of breasts.

Then, as the Termination Theme began, I felt them all untangling from me. Group Time was over.

"You really are Something Great!" Hearing My Girl's voice, I looked up to find her slipping out the door with My Old Buddy.

I was alone, relieved to be alone, but very lonely in the great empty Egg.

"Wait, My Good Dynamo!" It was Grouper Leader, sliding down into the Pit. He approached me formally, raised his hand, placed it upon my cheek, palm open, in a Grouper Gesture of Great Concern. "It must have hurt

[135]

you to see Your Old Buddy going off with Your Girl," he said.

"I told her our Dependency was coming to an end."

"Nonetheless . . . Rogar, you haven't been Looking Well or Acting Right. And I must say, it's a Bad Sign when you can lose a Dependent without letting yourself experience deep feelings of Hurt."

"I feel fine."

"That's your problem! You've got no reason to feel fine, none at all."

I am losing my capacity to Play these Games, and I stand very still, trying to think of a response.

"Should I suggest you see an Official? *I'd* feel better if you had a thorough Mood Evaluation."

"I'd like to help you feel better," I said.

Grouper Leader smiled gratefully, and I smiled back.

"It's just that I'm having a little trouble handling my feelings about My Girl."

"There, there . . . You'll get over it. And I won't have to take this any further, if you'll get yourself some help."

"Help?"

"Oh, nothing as serious as getting Capped."

I tried to show no fear.

"Not that I have anything against Capping," he said, "but it doesn't work so well with high-ranking Bureaucrats. Spoils initiative."

"I'm hardly disturbed enough to require any kind of surgery."

"And you probably don't feel far enough gone to admit yourself to a Pleasure Hospital."

[136]

"The whole idea amazes me! You haven't even seen me in weeks."

"Yes, but what does *that* mean? Has anyone been Keeping Tabs on you? I checked your Profile at NAMS, and you haven't been to any other Groups lately—unless you've been sneaking in without using your Mental Health Credit Card. Your Girl says she has no idea what's been happening to you, and you've been avoiding Buddy Checks for months. And there's only one record of a visit to a Pleasure Dome in half a year! Rogar, you've gone beyond Nondependency. You're acting damned near *In*dependent."

At least no hints about me and Gambol. No suggestions of Treason, no implications in the Official's death.

"It does sound like I need some help," I said. "I appreciate the Negative Feedback you're giving me."

"Now you've got the right idea! You had me worried, Rogar. Personally, I'd suggest you Take the Cure with an Autonomie. That's the sort of treatment for an intelligent Bureaucrat like yourself."

"I have thought about Autonomie Institute."

"Wonderful! I've been going myself. In fact, I'm in my sixth year."

"Your sixth year?"

"But My Autonomie tells me I'm almost ready to terminate. Anyway, it hasn't kept me from becoming a Grouper Leader."

"But *six years?*"

"Don't worry, it all goes on your Mental Health Credit Card."

[137]

"I see . . ."

"I was hoping you'd understand, Rogar. You're hardly the sort of fellow I'd want to see Capped, and Autonomie Institute is the wise man's alternative to Capping when he finds himself in trouble."

"Thank you," I said, making a smile.

He shook my hand and walked me to the door. "Meanwhile," he said as I left, "I'll be Keeping Tabs on you."

14th Entry

At the entrance to Autonomie Institute—an enormous round building of white pillars and dome that could have been a replica of the Oldtime Jefferson Memorial—I stood before the Electronic Monument.

Herein exist the Autonomies, Purified People so liberated that they can run off in their thoughts *ad infinitum* without inhibition by the slightest taint of GUILT, SHAME, and ANXIETY. They do it while they eat, for they are fed intravenously; and they do it while they sleep, for they have mastered sleep activities. After years of study and practice in Autonomie Institute, they have fulfilled that greatest NOW American Civil Right—the right to Free-associate!

Novitiates with special qualifications may enroll here to become Autonomies. Propitiates with no special qualifications may use their Mental Health Credit Cards to Pay for the Cure. And remember, "There's nothing shameful about Propitiation!"

We are unaffiliated with any other NOW Institution, and *all* Novitiates and Propitiates are completely protected by RAC—Relatively Absolute Confidentiality.

No one may tour here, and he who enters may be a long time gone.

Shaking with GUILT, SHAME, and ANXIETY, I slipped my Mental Health Credit Card into the slot and listened for the clicks that would instantly record my treatment on my profile in the National Information Pool at NAMS. Then I entered the door for Propitiates.

Inside I confronted a dozen other doors. I approached the one with a green light flashing above it; it vaporized and then materialized again behind me, trapping me in a closed cubicle.

The cubicle, body-tight, was growing darker. Neither the IN door nor the OUT door would vaporize! There was no way out except UP, and UP went off into blackness without stairs or a ladder.

The dim light was flickering.

Out it went!

Such a fool I've been to enter any NOW institution for help. What did I expect from NOW? I will Die at My Machine.

And what if they find my Journal?

Gambol, discovered and carried off to the Probe.

"Let me out of here!"

The total darkness summons an uneasy association. The Zoom Room Tomb? The Zoom Boom Room Womb Tomb? What kind of insanity is this?

Something from my CHILDHOOD.

The Zoom Boom Room?

"Help!"

The light flickered back on in a voice-pattern response.

[140]

"Hello?"
Nothing.
"Help!"
The light flickered again in response to my cry.
"Help. I need help!"
A recorded voice answered me:
"Now you're talking."

The light went on; the door in front of me opened toward the center of the Institute.

It was round and domed inside, like a Pleasure Dome, except that it was absolutely bare—no lights, scents, baths, undulating floors—no trappings of any kind under this great white ceiling many times the height of an Eggshell.

Hearing a muffled babbling I turned and saw a small withered man in the center of the great room. He was lying on a white slab of marble; an intravenous tube fed his arm, and words streamed from his mouth. Behind his head, there was a marble reclining chair. As I approached I saw a hole in the seat and a yellow caution light blinking in a porcelain basin beneath it.

This was *my* Autonomie!

As he chattered I picked up no hesitations, no blocks, no unexpressed ambivalences or doubts—not one private feeling. He was Disease-free!

"Ah, a person in need is a treat indeed. A growing young man with his mind all alert, a man with potential to grow and to know. A man I respect, a man I can help.

[141]

His presence is strong, his essence is bright, I'll fix up his mind and make him all right. I'll help him to find the freedom he seeks!"

With each phrase I felt tension leaving me.

His voice was trailing off now, and I leaned forward to hear:

"He thinks he's free, free to be, but he can't even ask for help. He can't even admit how human he is—how needy and lonely and crying for help. And he thinks he can make it without paying the fee, without paying society through a man such as me."

"Fee? But I used my Mental Health Credit Card."

"Yes, but you've got to Agree. You and me, we've got to Agree. AGREE."

"I don't understand. Agree to what?"

The old man smiled benevolently. "Why don't you tell me about yourself?"

"I don't know where to begin."

"Begin with your wish to free yourself of all Disease."

"I do seek freedom! Though I struggle with myself, My Autonomie, I feel as if I could be filled with a wonderful light. Sometimes I seem to step within the Light as if it glows from a Source greater than myself. Yet I feel that I am greater than myself, greater than the self I now know."

My Autonomie smiled again. "We all want to be Special," he said. "I have experience and age."

"Yes?"

"And I am covered with marvelous marble sores."

[142]

He raised one buttock and pointed, then eased himself down painfully. "I am, too."

I am?

Lurching forward, I fell upon the marble, cracking my kneecaps and letting out a yowl.

Something in me had been touched.

My Great Book Hallucination?

Could this man have insight into me?

But My Autonomie's mouth was opening and closing like a landed fish desperate for oxygen as he babbled on about marvelous marble sores and the girl who once sucked his pop and pulled his cock . . .

"Autonomie! Autonomie! *I am, too!*"

That stopped the old man.

He dragged himself up, supporting his head on one elbow, and, with a dying man's deliberation, told me:

"YOU ARE NOTHING BUT A FRAGMENT IN MY FREE ASSOCIATIONS!"

He fell back.

Never!

I am—

I cannot finish the thought.

An eerie warble echoed through the chamber. Astonished, I watched the old man pull out his intravenous tube, get up, and hobble over to the Pot like an invalid forced to fend for himself.

He bent over, scrutinized the empty Pot, then complained, "How can you expect me to predict the future if you won't give me anything to read?"

[143]

Walking out, he turned to me: "You get one Truism per hour, no more, no less, that is the rule. And you shall come three times a week until you Take the Cure."

As a caution light flashed over one of the exits, the warble grew louder, painfully loud to my ears. I rushed toward the exit. As I reached it, I realized that the entire circumference of the great round room was encircled by one exit door after another, and above each door was the word

EXIST

Or was it "exit"? I could not tell with the obscene yellow light and the painful warbling.

Now all the lights were flashing red and green and yellow, above the blurred signs.

I ran from the building, each door vaporizing before me. A *dozen doors* where once there were two or three.

I glanced up at the Electronic Monument and saw that one sentence was now underlined in red:

"There's nothing shameful about PROPITIATION."

15th Entry

These past few weeks I have become so preoccupied
with understanding My Autonomie that I have lacked
energy for my secret research.

And what about *her?* I cannot even think about her
any more.

Feeling drained of my creativity, I find myself
falling into exhaustion—and as my eyes close, against
my will, my Vision begins to come alive. I am bathed in
that glow richer than any sun I have known. But this
time I feel no book in my lap, no stone-heavy pages
slowly opening. Instead I seem to stand upright in a vast
open space of golden heat; yes, I stand alone in a great
desert.

This is the source of my Vision—ancient glowing
sands beneath a great orange sun! And there is a Voice
speaking to me, to this lone dark figure on a great
golden dune, and the Words are deep—deeper than my
Great Book Hallucination—and this time I hear the
Words:

WHO AM!

The light vanishes.

WHO AM?

Who is WHO AM?

Am I WHO AM?

I am WHO I AM?

WHO AM! is it a question, or an answer?

It is GOD who comes to Moses and says, "I AM WHO AM!"

And then Moses asks God, "What shall I tell Pharaoh?"

And God says, "Tell him WHO AM has sent you."

Has WHO AM sent me? Me? T. E. P. Rogar, O.B., O.B.P., NAMS? Sent me where and for what? To whom?

Gambol is the only one I want to be with.

But now, more than ever, that is too dangerous for us both.

I fall to my knees and speak words that fill me with Guilt, Shame, and Anxiety: "Dear God, I do not understand."

What am I doing on my knees?

I spring to my feet and stand in the middle of my empty, isolated Cube.

Words have been spoken to me, and I am speechless.

It has come to this: I can no longer carry on the dialogue alone, for I have things to say that I cannot say to myself.

An enormous pain wells up within me and I cry out:

Listen, Gambol
Listen, that I may speak . . .

As in lonely times in the past, my thoughts reach out across the centuries to the only man with whom I have ever felt at one, O. Peter Braggard. Tonight I opened up his last known work, *Memoirs of a Shameless Jew: Why I Resigned from Official Psychiatry.*

The title reflects the old man's unflagging pride in himself when, at the age of eighty-eight in the year 2024 (66 B.G.W.), he burned his American Psychiatric Association Card and his Mental Health Credit Card, thus subjecting himself to an Identity Card Crisis. An attempt was made to Cap him on the grounds that he had "forfeited his identity," and he was deprived of his Sound Mind/Sound Credit rating. But Official Psychiatry backed away from the scandal, and the old man was allowed to enter his tenth decade with an intact brain.

In the past it has been Braggard's outrage that has sustained me—his conviction that he knew the Truth and should speak it, no matter what the consequences—but lately I have begun to appreciate new aspects of his unique personality. Tonight, as I opened his *Memoirs,* I skipped over the pages of attack upon psychiatry and the pages of "alternatives" that no one would ever put into practice, and I found myself instead reading and rereading an odd little postscript to the book.

It seems that when the old man was in his nineties,

[147]

he sat down in the middle of the night and wrote this
little poem to his love of more than fifty years:

> Soft Touch, your Sunspots is on his way out;
> He leaves without Guilt, without Shame,
>   without a Doubt.
> His only uncertainty is where to die;
> Here at his typewriter, or there where you lie.
> But since we made love three times last night,
> I'll take my last breath where I fought the
>   good fight.

In fact, the old Braggard was not found Dead at his
Typewriter. He had crawled back into bed with his love
to spend another peaceful night upon her breast. The
actual date of either of their deaths is pure conjecture.
It is possible that they emigrated to Israel to "start a
new life" sometime during the fifth decade Before the
Good War.

I feel more tenderness for that Old Braggard at this
moment than I have ever felt, but it is a tenderness that
grows within another sentiment that borders on irritation.

I, too, would at this moment put my head upon *my*
sweet love's breast, if I could. And I admire his capacity
to fight against the abuses of his profession. It must
have been accomplished in the face of great fear, at least
in the beginning. But while Braggard was loving his
sweet woman and while he was carrying on his little war

with his colleagues, young Jews in America and Russia were giving their lives to save the Jews of Russia. Yes, while Russia was hoarding its Jews and then ransoming them to Israel, there were a few bold Americans who refused the Russian terms, who kidnapped Russian diplomats and ransomed *them,* who bombed Russian installations in America and cried out, "Never again!"

"Never again!" and yet again and again.

Even Braggard's attempts to warn against the dangers of psychiatry and brain technology seem somehow unsatisfying to me now. True, we have psycho-surgery and Capping today, just as he predicted. But before we could succumb to this, we had first to lose our individuality. And before we lost our individuality, our last remnants—the Jews, the Blacks, the Women, and the Human Beings—had to be overcome by brute force.

Where did Braggard stand when it came to arms? Where were all the intellectual Braggards of the Twentieth Century when countless unknown individuals were falling all around them?

I am who I am?

There is an undercurrent that runs almost unseen and unfelt beneath the ocean of history. It is the story of the Jew as Holy Warrior versus the Jew as Unholy Traitor. There were Jews who gave their lives to defeating the Nazis and to driving the British out of Palestine. Compared to them, the established Jewish leaders were collaborators, traitors who rubbed elbows and made deals with the destroyers of Jews throughout the world.

The Jewish leaders of the Twentieth Century did little more to prevent the slaughter of the six million than did the British, the Russians, and the Americans. Israel itself was nursed to life with the blood of the six million—for the future leaders of Israel joined in the conspiracy of silence to protect their political positions with the Allies. Worse, these future leaders of Israel tried to destroy men like Ze'ev Jabotinsky, who sought to arouse the six million to fight back. Still worse, when the Holocaust was upon the Jews of Europe, the future leaders of Israel openly collaborated with the Nazis to free "prominent Jews," in return for which they made sure the six million went duped and leaderless to the death camps. And finally, still selling their fellow Jews to secure their own political supremacy, they collaborated with the British against the Jewish Freedom Fighters—the Holy Warriors of the Irgun and the Stern Group—who nonetheless drove the British out of Palestine.

I have read Jewish Authorities from the Twentieth Century who claim that Moses himself acted too rashly when he smote the Egyptian he found beating a fellow Jew.

The Maccabees against the Greeks. The Zealots against the Romans. The Irgun and Sternists against the British. The Hebrew Defense League against the Russians, the Arab terrorists, and American anti-Semites. Each

[150]

met more deadly opposition from the Jewish Establishment than from the enemy.

But I am no Holy Warrior.

What *is* my preoccupation with Jews? With Israel?

Do I have a shred of evidence that I am Jewish?

Every man in the Western World has Jewish blood either in his veins or on his hands, and all too many have both. This seems certain after their thousands of years upon the earth. Yet I don't have so much as a hint that anyone else in America thinks of himself as a Jew.

Nor am I even sure that Jewishness is the issue. It has something more to do with Individualism.

I wouldn't know where to begin finding others to join me in a Holy War to save the Individuals of America from extinction.

But I am who I am, and I have Visions . . .

Perhaps I seek this prophetic role to escape something more frightening. There were self-appointed prophets in the Twentieth Century, too: like Buber, who wrote of "I and Thou" and intimated that God Himself had given him his words, perhaps to explain the fact that they were largely unintelligible. Buber, who loved everyone but would fight for no one.

Does the death of the Official make me a Terrorist?

I would have killed the man outright if Gambol hadn't stopped me.

But that was reflexive self-defense. It proves that my instincts remain intact despite NOW America, but it hardly signifies the courage and idealism required to join

[151]

in a Holy War with whatever Individuals may still exist. Braggard himself glimpsed enough of this to write:

> In the beginning, God made each of us.
> In the end, we must make ourselves.
> We must do it together.

But with whom? And how?

16th Entry

As My Autonomie lay upon his marble slab, pale urine bubbled slowly through a catheter and into an open bottle on the floor—more evidence of life than I usually see from him.

He blinked occasionally, and I noticed one fine pulsation in his flesh-ringed neck; another in the crease of his inner arm near the bruise marks where his IV needle is inserted.

A fine lip movement, too, as if mouthing something he was memorizing; but his eyes were fixed on the bare dome of the Institute.

As I approached him he began to mutter. "I may seem old, but I resonate and resound like a fine violin. I feel his feelings in my bones and in my sinews. I feel his struggles to free and to find himself. I move toward him with My Spirit, my spirit as supple as my body is old. My heart takes flight to lead him from himself to his new Freedom."

Such eloquence!

[153]

"My Autonomie, I will try my best to let you help free me. I am feeling stronger today, strong enough to know that I must be something more to you than a Fragment in your Free Associations. I can tell your Associations are about me and about my Freedom, I know that something is taking place here and that we are having an impact upon each other. I can tell you that I have had a profound Vision since we were last together."

A single bubble jumped in the catheter.

Sometimes the old man seems Tuned In to me!

"Listen, My Autonomie. I AM WHO AM. Do you understand? No matter what you think about me, I AM WHO AM!"

Something has happened.

It's silent in here—he's stopped talking!

He lifts his shoulder an inch off his slab and grimaces.

"Are you in pain, My Autonomie?"

"This isn't MY therapy!" He says it with youthful timbre. And then, except for his fishmouth motion, he again becomes as still as the motion of decay.

I watch his life escaping through his mouth, his body shriveling with the flight of his last energy.

I have to tell him!

"I've heard a Voice."

His lower belly jumps; a bubble leaps another inch down the tube.

"I felt like a Hebrew Prophet."

[154]

Gas pains? An internal rumination? Something crosses his face.

"Suppose I decide there's nothing crazy about being a Hebrew Prophet? Suppose I decide that my Illness is my Identity?"

There's a rush of piss back *up* the tube.

I decide where to draw the line on my confessions. I will not say a word about Gambol, no matter what.

"You don't trust me," he announces.

"I'm sorry. I really am. If anything, I wish I could reach out to you."

"But you don't trust me."

He props himself up on one elbow and stares at me like a physician puzzling over an oddity. Then he shrugs hard, slumps back, and resumes his muttering.

"I'm glad you're reacting to me, Autonomie, even if you seem insulted."

He sighed.

A man at the end of his patience? Perhaps I have been Making Up his feelings.

"Autonomie, there is one thing I have to know from you before I can go on."

He keeps muttering, a little louder now.

"My question is this—can you promise me that no one will ever hear a word of what I am telling you here?"

He clears his throat. "Aaaaahhh-GRAGGLE!" Then, "My Propitiate, RAC is the one and only thing I can promise you in life—*Relative Absolute Confidentiality.*"

[155]

And then I blurt it out:

"I'm Chief Historian for the Twentieth Century, but secretly I write my own history. I study myself and America, and more and more, I find myself investigating IT—yes, IT!—THE HEBREW DISEASE."

He does not flinch.

"My studies are going beyond NOW—beyond *all* Official History into my own understanding of life!"

"Ah, youth!"

"What are you talking about? I'm more than thirty years old!"

"I was only beginning my most important training at thirty. But you do very well for your age."

"I *am* just a Fragment in your Free Associations. But I am finding myself within myself. I AM WHO AM!"

"Oh, really?" He raises one eyebrow. "That's what I thought you said at the beginning of the Hour. It's from the Old Bible, isn't it?"

He knows the Old Bible?

"And as I recall," he says, "it is GOD who declares to Moses, I AM WHO AM. Have you become GOD?"

He asks it offhandedly, as if he's simply curious.

"I don't mean it that way."

"Can you say what you mean?" His tone is sympathetic.

"I mean I AM WHO I AM. Yes, that's it—I Am Who *I* am!"

"And that gives you the right to dismiss Official History with a flourish of your hand? To stand above

[156]

NOW America? I am who I am, too. And so are a lot of other people. But how can you stand above America and Official Knowledge?"

"Anybody can. It's easy."

"No one has ever said that it's *difficult* to be wrong. But who has chosen *you* to Make Up Life in Your Own Head?"

"I am free, Autonomie."

"And I am Liberated, too!" he shouted. "I Free-associate!"

"Autonomie, I am quitting therapy. It is time for me to leave you."

He leaped up. "Leave me? Leave me?" He was screaming. "How dare you leave me? You have not *Taken the Cure!*"

"What are you talking about?"

"The AGREEMENT! We must agree when it is time for you to go. We must AGREE about your cure. Without that there is nothing!"

"But *why?*"

"If you weren't sick you would understand that we must AGREE."

"No. Never!" I cried out in hurt, fear, uncertainty. *"No* man should wait upon another man's judgment. My judgment is absolutely my own!"

"Nothing is Absolute." That tone from my CHILD-HOOD: grave, foreboding. "That you strive for Absolutes is another part of your Illness. There are many Facets to your Illness. Look how frightened and confused you feel right now. And you want to leave!"

[157]

"But the woman I love, we *both* believe in these Absolutes."

"I have My Girl, too, and we love each other." His eyes became glassy as he assumed Free-Association Posture in the middle of the floor. "My Girl sucks my cock, burns my warts, empties my bladder bag, and rubs my marble sores, and I am Your Autonomie, and you have made my catheter back up and my bladder is too full, and I have been Free-associating for thirty years, and he thinks in Absolutes, he who is so proud of His Girl and who talks about writing and going beyond NOW and leaving me before the Agreement, running from Insight and Acting Out against me, he who is nothing more than a Fragment in my Free Associations, he will decide all for himself, decide all, decide all, all, ball, cock, suck, oh, ho! My Girl! My Girl!"

"You're talking crazy!"

"You are making me talk crazy by refusing to accept me as Your Autonomie." His tone is deliberate, rational.

A sorrowful warbling echoed through the Dome, signaling the end of my hour. I stared at him, but he was Free-associating about his youth and His Girl; I was no longer even a Fragment in his Free Associations.

I started to leave, but every single light over every exit was blinking RED, and all the EXIST signs now read NO EXIT.

I walked right through them, anyway.

[158]

17th Entry

If My Autonomie is an Official, he will turn me in as soon as he's sure that I'm not coming back to him. But I have exhausted all sources of information about the Autonomie, except the direct approach—an inquiry into my NAMS Q Tube.

Feeling as if I were Living in the Shadow of the Eye, I Touched Toned my inquiry into the Tube: "What is the relationship between Oldtime Psychiatry, Psycho-analysis, and the Autonomies? Are the Autonomies Officials?"

I waited for the fatal Printout telling me to turn myself in to an Official.

Instead, My Boss's animated facsimile materialized on the screen.

"I'm sorry, Rogar, but this question is delicate in nature. Are your motives strictly public? Not a hint of the private? Think it over for a moment."

I took a moment. Then, "Strictly public, sir."

"What problem are you investigating?"

"The relationship between Autonomies and Officials. I believe there is considerable confusion about this in the minds of most NOW Americans."

There was a delay, a fraction of a second, long enough to indicate that special circuitry was required to find the next animated answer:

"Did it occur to you that this 'confusion' may be at the heart of NOW American Faith?"

"Sir, if this question is Inappropriate, I withdraw it."

"Your discretion is reassuring. You may make further direct inquiries of William A. Smith, NICMHMS."

In a few minutes I disembarked at NICMHMS, and after a Mental Health Credit check, I was allowed to advance through an electronic barrier to meet William A. Smith, so identified by a name plaque casually balanced on his head.

Five feet tall and three feet wide, he was colored the usual institutional green with one round Q-tube Screen at eye level in his square head. He had no visible controls, only a mouth slot for my Card.

"Please state your request as succinctly as possible."

"What is the relationship between Oldtime psychiatry, Oldtime psychoanalysis, the Autonomies, and the Officials?"

"Your request is an unusual one. Most Americans don't really care."

"Should I withdraw it?"

"No, there is no secret about the relationship between them. It has always been so plain, one wonders why the most casual observer could have doubts about it."

"They are all the same!"

"Of course. With exceptions."

William A. Smith and I stared silently at each other, until I could ask calmly, "Please elaborate on the relationships and the exceptions."

"The purpose of Oldtime psychiatry was the control of the individual in the interest of the group." He was reciting practically verbatim from the work of O. Peter Braggard; so one generation's cynicism became another's truth. "Mental Hospitalization, drugs, electro-shock, psychosurgery, and directive, authoritarian psychotherapy were among its methods."

"But psychoanalysis? Was that a part of psychiatry?"

"Founded by the Jew Freud, psychoanalysis sought to 'liberate' the individual from the group. Freud refuted psychiatry, and psychiatry threw Freud out. To his dying day, Freud resisted psychiatry's later attempts to take over psychoanalysis. He warned his disciples to stay clear of psychiatry and to isolate themselves in Psychoanalytic Institutes. He used none of the standard psychiatric treatments, and he instructed his disciples to fear those physicians who sought to make psychoanalysis a branch of medicine and psychiatry. But within a decade of Freud's death, psychiatry succeeded in taking over psychoanalysis. The Group must always triumph. Freud, being a Jew, was incapable of understanding that."

"And the Autonomies and the Officials?"

"When the National Agency for Mental Security was created, combining the Mental Health and Police functions of the state in one invincible authority, it was discovered that psychiatry had already been performing these functions on a smaller scale. So the psychiatrist became a specialized Official under the authority of NAMS. Since nearly all psychoanalysts were already psychiatrists, they too became specialized Officials, called Autonomies."

"Having all powers and duties of Officials?"

"With one exception. The Autonomie is bound by RAC—Relative Absolute Confidentiality."

I waited, and so did Smith.

"What does 'Relative Absolute' mean?"

"It means that special exceptions must be reported to NAMS."

"Like what?"

"The Autonomie, like the psychoanalyst before him, will break confidentiality when there is a Clear and Present Danger."

"To whom?"

"To anyone."

"Then what happens?"

"That depends on the Autonomie's recommendation. Involuntary Grouper devotions. Behavioral Modification Therapy. Directive Psychotherapy. Pleasure Hospitalization. Drugs. Capping, as a last resort. The Pleasure Probe in cases of treason."

"The Autonomies sound exactly like Twentieth-century Psychiatrists."

"*They* didn't have the Pleasure Probe," Smith said curtly. "At least, they had not perfected it and adapted it for political control."

[162]

"But there's no other difference."

"Hardly the case, Rogar. The Official represents a major reform over the Twentieth-century psychiatrist and psychoanalyst. The Official can't make a personal profit based upon the number of people he brings under his power. Nor can he apply this power to anyone he chooses. It is hard to believe that an advanced society left such potentially destructive technologies in the hands of individual men, particularly when those men were often in the pay of institutions or families hostile to the person being treated—hostile to the point of wanting to be rid of him at any cost. Such an exercise of personal power over other individuals is inconceivable in NOW America. That is why we no longer have psychiatrists, and that is why our Officials are held responsible to NAMS."

"And the Autonomies also report cases of treason?"

"Yes, but the prophylactic function of the Autonomie is more important. The Autonomies, like the psychoanalysts and psychiatrists before them, are charged with the task of preoccupying and distracting potential Radicals and Revolutionaries, particularly those suffering from traces of the Hebrew Disease. The Autonomies offer them Free Association as a substitute for more dangerous Political Freedoms."

William A. Smith's belly lamp showed that he was at rest, that I need pursue the interview no further.

At least I haven't mentioned Gambol's name to My Autonomie.

But I have done what I must do. I have left My Autonomie before submitting to him.

[163]

I can only hope he sees me as no potential threat to NOW America, and will wait for me to return to him like any NOW American suffering from Simpleminded Dependency.

Meanwhile, all my energy must go into verifying whether or not Israel exists.

18th Entry

Israel lives!

At least, it survived the Good War.

My source is the *Diary of the Chief Bugger's Distraught Housewife,* a document that spans the period of our preparations for the Good War, as well as several decades after. Apparently her renown as a patriot discouraged censorship, for I have here my first eyewitness account of the day After the Good War.

The key to our victory was the MICROBOMB, a Subnuclear Obliviation device which brings Antimatter into sudden confrontation with Matter, causing an explosion that unleashes God's Original Universal Power (GOUP), the very stuff which generates the universe. The BOMB causes chain reactions within the Earth itself, dwarfing nuclear fission, producing secondary earthquakes, turning everything to GOUP, and, incidentally, hastening universal entropy.

The Microbombs, small enough to be carried in a satchel, were easily planted abroad during normal diplomatic contact with each of the nuclear powers: China, Japan, United Europe, White Africa, and Israel. Then, by remote control, we detonated all of them at once and turned each of the world's great powers into GOUP.

Overkill became a formality, but our Mop-up Rockets would not be denied their moment, and they were unleashed upon the remainder of the world, including Cuba, that "thorn in our geographic groin."

The night after our Victory, a celebration was gathered in the now abandoned White House. But until NOW there has been no explanation why the President moved out of the White House and established himself in the Presidential Towers, a great White Column rising from the midst of the Pentagon Garden.

Here are the eyewitness details from the *Diary of the Chief Bugger's Distraught Housewife:*

January 1st, the Year 1, A.G.W., 10 A.M.:

I still can't believe it! Everything was going so well at the Presidential War Ball. The orchestra was playing, and everyone was bubbling with excitement and enthusiasm. Aerial photographs on the ceiling depicted the Obliviation of our enemies, including the quiet Caribbean Sea where Cuba had been. There were colorful posters: NOW BELONGS TO AMERICA, and THIS IS THE YEAR ONE, A.G.W., and CUBA IS A FISHING SHOAL, and THEY SAID ISRAEL COULDN'T LOSE A WAR. There was another whole wall where you could write anything you wanted, and someone had printed "God must be on Our Side because there is No Other

[166]

Side." Even my husband, who's ferreted out subversives from every corner of America, was boasting that America would never again need an FBI or CIA or NSA or PIG. And nobody even noticed THAT AWFUL LITTLE MAN!

The President was explaining how we'd finally "gotten even" with the United Nations and *all* the other Nations and how clever we were to have invented those amazing MICROBOMBS. Then that LITTLE MAN jumped into the middle of the floor and opened his jacket; and instead of a big belly he pulled out this thing, the size of a medicine ball but black and with long spikes sticking out and a BIG RED BUTTON. He said he could press the Button and set off a Subnuclear Obliviation and "regenerate the United States. I'll turn you all to GOUP and give GOD a second chance to *make* something out of you!"

As if God wasn't on OUR side!

Everyone looked at the President to see if it was a joke, only he was scowling like somebody had hit him in the mouth with a horseshoe. And then the President was looking at General Joint, and General Joint was nodding, Yes, to show it *did* look like a MICROBOMB.

And then this little man is telling us he's a JEW.

He's admitting it, without anyone even asking him.

A JEW at the Presidential WAR BALL!

And if that isn't bad enough, he's the ex-Israeli Ambassador, "ex-" because the only proper thing was to do away with all the ambassadors after we'd done away with their countries. I could see from my husband's face that he was going to give hell to the agent in charge of Ambassador Assassinations.

The little JEW was saying that it was too late to do anything. Israel had watched US plant every Microbomb there, and then Hebrew Agent-Priests had flown them right back here and hidden them all over America. With

[167]

one push of a button in Jerusalem, the East Coast and the West Coast would crack and slide into the oceans, and everything in the middle would be turned to GOUP. That's what he said! And he was talking in perfect English, like he'd learned it in an English prep school, and telling US that it would be God's punishment for our sins, as if we hadn't won the War fair and square.

He explained that Israel was hardly damaged, that knocking out our Mop-up Rockets had been easy. Once the dust clouds settled from the plowed-up Arab Lands, he said, Israel would be found glistening beneath the sun.

He warned us not to do anything rash, because at stake was the difference between an American Continent and a Puddle of GOUP. Then he put the BOMB down in the middle of the floor "for all time, so the White House will at last generate Peace on Earth."

That horrible little man!

He told General Joint to escort him to the Presidential Rocket Pad and fly him back to Israel in Air Force One. He stuck out his elbow, and General Joint took it and escorted him out as free as could be.

It was *so* quiet for a few seconds, and we all stared at our President, who was looking hangjaw at the Bomb, like he was losing the Big Game of His Life and didn't even dare touch the ball. I wanted to give him a little hug and a peck. But then our President was dashing across the floor like a broken field runner, almost knocking over the BOMB on his way out of the Ballroom; and everyone was breaking out through windows, pushing down the doors to the terrace and climbing over tables and each other, and the floor was shaking, and I thought maybe *that* would set off The Bomb, and I started running too, losing one of my slippers and turning my ankle, and it was horrible, it was horrible, it was horrible, just when everything was going so fine, it was horrible, and all because of that little man.

[168]

Oh, why did God have to make Jews!

So the White House was precipitously abandoned and boarded up. But does the ballroom still enshrine a Microbomb throbbing to the touch of an Israeli finger in far-off Jerusalem?

And if Israel does exist, does it control more than the Arab Lands? And could a man with the Hebrew Disease flee to Israel for his cure? Or is Israel the Source but not the Cure?

The "Source" of what? Disease? Truth? Death? Love?

Whatever, Israel is now my one hope—*our* one hope.

This hope increases with my second find—a later document tucked inside the *Diary of the Chief Bugger's Housewife.*

Date:	November 22, 19 A.G.W.
Clearance:	TOP SECRET
From:	Office of Jewish Affairs Bureau of Conquered Lands
To:	Office of the Attorney General
Subject:	Status Report Activities of Hebrew Agent-Priests
File Code:	JEW-A/P-C.L.

Hebrew Agent-Priests armed with vials of Jewish Tears are found everywhere proselytizing in the Conquered Lands, whose devastation has made them fertile grounds for the messianic message that the vengeful God who has punished man now offers redemption. America may have won the Good War at the cost of surrounding itself with Jews!

Remember that the mighty Roman Empire fell before the diluted C-Strain form of the Hebrew Disease, and then consider what it means that we are now surrounded by the Real Thing! By "H" Itself!

Nor can we attack Israel directly, for the Jews have raised an electronic curtain around Southern Europe, North Africa, and the Middle East; their so-called Shield of God, which if breached will automatically set off the Microbombs they have planted in America. In twenty years, we have only accounted for three of a possible dozen Microbombs: the one in the boarded-up White House, another found in the eye of the now abandoned Statue of Liberty, a third in the now closed Football Hall of Fame inside the gilded Game Ball from the 1976 Centennial Super Bowl.

Our own electronic curtain protects us from propaganda beamed toward Americans, but the Jews freely broadcast messages like this to the Conquered Lands:

There is no truth except God's and all God's truth resides in Each Man and Each Woman. And Each shall answer to God and to himself; and none shall answer to Other Men or to the Group. And Each shall worship God in himself: and none shall worship Another Man or the Group. And all the world is ONE, and shall worship none except THE ONE. And all these truths are Absolute, as is Each Man, each Absolute in being ONE.

The aftermath of the War must have transformed Israel from just another power-loving mini-empire into the Kingdom of Priests promised in the Bible:

The LORD will establish you as His holy people, as He swore to you, if you keep the commandments of the LORD your God and walk in His ways. And all the

[170]

peoples of the earth shall see that the LORD'S name is proclaimed over you, and they shall stand in fear of you.

For out of Zion shall go forth the law, and the word of the LORD from Jerusalem. He shall judge between the nations, and shall decide for many peoples. . . .

I will give you as a light to the nations, that my salvation may reach the end of the earth.

Listen to me, quoting the Bible like a Jew!

19th Entry

Gambol wants to see me again!

My Bubble frolics through the night, doing turns and flips in the empty skyway, a bright ball of light spinning along in the darkness, responding not to my fingertip controls but to my commands—no, to my thoughts and feelings, to my whole spirit!

I float suspended above Gambol's Stack of Cubes, then down, slowly, toward her Pad. At my verbal instruction, "J. A. R. D. Gambol," the Chute begins a slow graceful crawl around the outside of her Stack, stopping at her porch.

I found her standing inside her open Cube.

We sat down together without a word, and I grew weak trying to focus my blurring vision on her face.

She put her hand on my shoulder; her hand trembled, and my shoulder shook.

I leaned over, nearly falling forward, and kissed her tears, tasted their salt and knew that nothing in this woman could harm me. We rested against each other, as much to prop each other up as to hold.

[173]

My pike was erect and throbbing to the beat of my heart, swelling like a great ache between us.

"You want my body so much?" she whispered.

"More. And I want you Without the Bag."

I fumbled and found her, and she wrapped her great legs about me and took me within her.

My cock flesh melted away within her cunt, her cunt fleshing to my cock, and I poured myself into her with a groan.

Then I lay still upon her as her body quieted beneath me.

We had hardly spoken.

Was that why I felt so unsatisfied?

I could not believe that making love without the Bag came to nothing more than this.

I looked up from her breast and into her face. "Gambol?"

She did not answer.

An image of lying upon a great wounded animal. "Gambol!"

Her eyes trembled, straining to open.

"Be with me!" I begged.

"With whom?"

I held her close in my arms and felt her body relax little by little. Then I curled up, still halfway on top of her, a child within the crook of her soft arm and round shoulder, and I began to doze off.

The hitch in her breathing woke me—small sucks of air as if stifling an emotion, the way children are taught to hold back their tears.

[174]

Children? CHILDHOOD?

My love takes Pain to sleep with her—the Pain of CHILDHOOD!

She was still whimpering, quite loudly now, but deep within sleep. Is this why she lives and sleeps alone? Does she cry herself to sleep, Spreading Tears every time she goes to bed?

And some of the whimpering noises are the same sounds she made when I entered her.

I shook her shoulders in my hands, and she cried aloud in her sleep: "Rogar! Gambol! Rogar! Gambol!"

"My love?"

"I'm in the ROOM!" she called out.

My ribs shook like broken wings.

It was many minutes before she opened her eyes, looked me straight in the face, and said, "Who's there?"

I repeated my name, helplessly.

"But who's inside?"

I reached over and laid my palm upon her cheek and told her as strongly as I could, "I love you. Let my love overcome your fear."

"It's not just *my* fear," she told me.

"I don't know what you mean."

My body ached; my joints felt hot with Guilt, Shame, and Anxiety.

"I can't help you, Gambol." I held my hands cupped before my face, crying into them.

I, T. E. P. Rogar, had come up against the limits of my power. I could not break through to Gambol, could not rescue her from her Pain.

[175]

I sat beside her for a long time as she lay upon the floor with her eyes closed, her face and hair wet, her body damp from us.

"I don't understand," I told her when she opened her eyes.

She did not smile or try to relieve my distress. Instead she said, in a clear and simple voice, "You forgot that I'm a human being."

"Like the woman who was burned to death?"

"Not a Card-carrying Human Being. But I don't want your help, Rogar. I want you to love yourself so that you can love me."

The effort to control my fear kept me silent.

"Rogar, did you read the history of the Human Beings?"

"Yes, but I'm not like those men who burned the girl."

"Rogar, the history of the Human Beings is not about men. It's about women."

"But it ended with the men—"

"No, it ended with a *woman* living to the very last for her own truths."

My fear gave way to astonishment.

"Why did you come back to me?" she asked gently.

"Many confused reasons. But I know I need you to keep on discovering myself."

"That's why I need you."

I waited to hear more.

"After the death of the Official on the mountain,"

[176]

she said, "I realized that he had nearly escaped, because of me."

"I thought it was your tenderness that made you stop me from killing him."

"That's what I thought, until you said to me, 'The life in us killed him.' Then I understood why you wanted to do it—because you valued our lives and our right to live."

We sat silently again for a few minutes.

"What did you do after we left each other?" I asked.

"I've been keeping to myself as much as I can without arousing suspicion. And for the first time in my life, I've been painting a great many self-portraits. I've begun to find the things in myself that you have found in me—strength, tenderness, value. When I became convinced that I could value myself even when you might lapse—then I felt ready to see you again."

"But you waited for me to call you."

"I knew that as a man you'd need more time."

"I suppose I'm still too much a Dynamo to accept that. It's ridiculous, I know."

"It's been done to you, Rogar. As a man, you think you have much more than women can ever have. So it takes you longer to find the emptiness in all that's offered you. For me, the options were few. Once I had tried going into the Bag with a Dynamo, I had tested and exhausted all the alternatives for women in America."

We sat quietly, becoming used to each other again. I

[177]

thought especially of the night we first painted and wrote together.

"I want to make love with you, Rogar, but very carefully. Every time we lie down with each other from now on, it will be a deeper reaching into ourselves."

We lay down on our sides and touched each other's faces.

"When you were in me the first time tonight, Rogar, you came into me only as deep as my fear goes. I want you deeper."

"I went only as far as my own fear would let me go. I want to go much deeper."

She gently turned me on my back and put her tongue into my mouth, searching back into my throat until I opened and let her fill me. She placed her finger deep between my buttocks and gently widened me; she found the tunnel of my balls; and she placed her mouth upon my pike and sweetly pushed her tongue against its eye until even my most tender lips admitted her. She loosened me, opened me, reached into me, and I felt all the muscles that close my body slowly parting to her touch.

Now my lips and tongue found her, and every part of her turned to feeling within my mouth; her body shivering and prickling with new pleasures. Her ears, her nose, her mouth, her eyes, and all the places between her thighs opened up to me. Her breasts grew larger, her nipples glistened from my lips. Her vagina's bud swelled within my mouth, became plump and seemed to burst into juice with the gentle pressure of my tongue.

[178]

She called out to me, and I helped her to raise me above her body. I seemed to float there, waiting for her to catch me within her arms and legs. Then my pike grew to meet our strength, and her body opened up large enough for us both. We entered into a great darkness; we trembled and grew afraid and then looked into each other's faces—I saw my love and my love saw me—and the Golden Light came upon us. We rode within its warmth and ascended to our first coming.

20th Entry

Across from me there is a patch of brown turning black in the night like a birthmark on the mountain's side, the place where the Official died.

I fix my feet more firmly on the great rock above the valley, but it rumbles beneath me, as if the small Capsule of my Journal could explode and overturn my pedestal in the darkness.

Any thought, any feeling pursued to its own end will drive a man into places no one can go with him. Perhaps that is why Gambol and I both need to be alone tonight after so many nights together.

But I can no more guess what she is facing by herself on her balcony than I can guess what is happening with me upon the mountain.

Unless it is about CHILDHOOD.

I keep having feelings about CHILDHOOD when I make love with her. It is as if our lovemaking defies all the lessons locked away in my amnesia.

I sit down on the ledge, dangling my legs some fifty feet above the mountain's dark slope.

An intruder behind me could end my uncertainty for all time.

Would someone a thousand years from now find my Journal beneath the rock—a Time Capsule for the next millennium?

If I distribute it now, Gambol and I will have to take flight from America. But if I wait much longer before completing it, we will both be caught.

I could disguise Gambol's identity in the Journal. That might give her the option of staying behind. But there's no disguising her without destroying her—and no disguising her without disguising me. I would end up with nothing where once there were a man and a woman.

I stand up on the rock, strong in the presence of myself and Gambol.

I am alone, but not alone. I am in the company of all others who have tried to face the Source.

Those Ancient Hebrews facing God, quaking with fear, facing the One. No wonder God hid Himself within a cloud. To see Him is too much for any man who cannot bear to see himself.

The Golden Glow is upon me! The light of my Hallucinations, the light of my love for Gambol. I stand tall upon the great rock above the valley, alone and radiating, and I speak words aloud, my own Great Book opening within me; and the words are mine and yet they are not mine. I draw them from this moment even as they arise from all time:

I am Rogar, the last Hebrew in America, speaking to

you in the Year 112 After the Good War, and I do not know for whom I speak unless WHO AM has sent me.

Here in America, the Final Solution has come, not through a policy of exterminating Jews but through the destruction of the idea of A MAN.

I believe that I am chosen, I AM WHO I AM, and I partake of WHO AM and WHAT IS. I know because I have discovered this within myself.

This bag of flesh that hangs between my legs is no mere NOW repository for the juices of pleasure; it is a treasury of Individuals. Each seed within me has been passed on from man to man and woman to woman through millennia—seeds of the One, seeds of individuals who partake of the One.

I take up the obligations of the Chosen Ones who choose THE ONE, and I oppose all that goes on NOW and has gone on throughout all time in opposition to the Individual.

Tonight will be my first night alone within the mountains and the woods, and I climb down to stretch out upon a soft bed of pine needles. Near my head beneath the rock the Capsule copy of my Journal rests as safely as within the heart of the mountain itself.

And then it happens: I begin to recall my CHILD-HOOD.

21st Entry

I had a very good CHILDHOOD, because I was my
mother's favorite and because my father gave me values.
My mother would look at her other children and then
take me aside and say, "You'll outdo them all, son.
You'll always be my favorite." I did do well—so well
that I became the Best Child in the House, and one year
I was voted

> Best all around
> Most likely to succeed
> Cocksucker of all
> For my age.

Mother was so proud of me when I got home that
she said to me, "Son, if you were only taller, you'd be
perfect." But my father said, "Don't give the kid ideas.
He can brag when they give him medals."

So I went out for track and I became

> The shortest, fattest, fastest
> Runner in the School
> Of all time.

And they gave me medals; but my father had forgotten that he ever wanted them.

At my graduation I received awards for Top Ten, Outstanding Competitor, Editor, and President. But someone else in the House was named

> Best all around
> Most likely to succeed
> Cocksucker of all
> In the Graduating Class.

And my mom was very hurt for me, and she told me that the school Officials were jealous because I was her favorite.

I was my mother's favorite!

This meant a lot to me—I knew I'd never have a chance to make it into the Elite of Industry or Government, because Mom and Dad were too busy helping the other children get ahead.

> But I learned to love Mom and Dad
> Because they were my parents.
> And that made me ready
> To become a Bureaucrat.

Then at last Dad came through for me. It was Career Day, the first time he'd come to school with me, and it was time for the Big Initiation after Graduation.

How I remember looking up to him that day: Dad with his carefully groomed hair and the touch of gray where his temples were growing thinner, Dad with the laugh wrinkles in the corners of his eyes, Dad with his shadow of a beard that was always dark and raspy, Dad with his large warm hand on my head as I bowed my head down to suck him.

"Suck, suck, my little son."

I cherish the memory of his hand upon me. It was the only time he ever touched me lovingly.

Mom said he had trouble showing his feelings.

The rest of Career Day is easy to recall, coming as it does in the borderland between CHILDHOOD and adulthood. Probably most of my readers will remember their own experiences with little difficulty. After we had satisfied our parents and the friends of our parents from the neighboring Houses, our teachers lined up. Next came recruiters from Industry and Government, ready to compare us with other recent crops of little Cocksuckers. And then we were prepared to go down before the stalwarts of our society: the guardians of our morality, the Official Psychiatrists, and the guardians of our culture, the Official Critics of the Arts and Literature.

That's why my readers may remember this expression from CHILDHOOD: "He'll suck Psychiatrists." It describes anyone who seems destined to make an Exceptional Adjustment to NOW America. And also the expression, "He'll suck Critics," to designate anyone who shows unusual aptitude for the Arts and Literature. Indeed, it is said, "A man who can suck a Critic can suck anyone."

[187]

But as often as we were supposed to suck adults, I remember that we were not allowed to suck among ourselves.

They called me Timmy, in the House of Ridicule Without Love:

"Don't mess, don't cry, smile!, and don't touch yourself, Timmy."

"Go to sleep, wake up, don't wet yourself, don't soil yourself, smile!, and don't touch yourself."

"Say Mommy, say Daddy, do what you're told, smile!, and don't touch yourself."

"Stop crying, wear your clothes, stay in line, say thank you, don't talk, smile!, and don't touch yourself."

"Sit in your chair, do your studies, don't stare, be nice, don't talk back, smile!, and don't touch yourself."

"Don't *ever* do that, Timmy!"

Once they caught a little boy and girl playing with each other and it went very badly for them. I can't remember exactly what they did to them. Something about the ZOOM BOOM ROOM.

My memories fade again.

I struggle to hang on to what I have already recalled.

Then I remember the Principle I formulated for myself to sum up everything that was being done to me:

> Parents are to keep children
> from touching.

I did not dare tell this to anyone, but I scratched it on tiny pieces of film and hid them all over the House and outdoors and at school. If anyone found them, I never heard about it. But I swore I would remember.

Thus I primed myself to recall my CHILDHOOD in my adulthood.

But there is something else to remember.

Something to do with my Journal research.

Something I stole.

I stole *research material.* I took a Career Day Pamphlet from one of the parents. Knowing I was already entering amnesia for my CHILDHOOD, I spent a month committing it to memory.

AN OFFICIAL HISTORY
OF
FAMILY LIFE IN AMERICA

There is no better time than Career Day for parents to recall the history of American Family Life.

Before the Good War, families lived together—mothers, fathers, and children—in their own private homes all over America. Within each home the parents possessed powers beyond those of any dictator—complete liberty to do anything to the growing young minds, hearts, and bodies of their children.

As a result, the Misery of CHILDHOOD was almost universal, though its particular form varied from one home to another. In some homes the children were ridiculed unmercifully without redeeming love. In others they were beaten and then made to feel guilty for causing their parents to beat them; or deprived and then made to believe they deserved their deprivations. In others the children were raised in isolation, and taught to believe this was only natural. In still others the children were forced to work endlessly toward ever

[189]

greater achievements without a thought to what they wanted for themselves.

Hardly anyone was concerned about the severity of these conditions within the typical American Family, and no one sponsored any attempts at reform. And even among those who had some understanding of the Misery, none grasped its importance as a prerequisite for American Adulthood. No one appreciated the Necessity of Misery in CHILDHOOD because no one understood what the children would otherwise *do!*

In the period of breakneck political reform After the Good War, America suddenly awoke to the facts of life about CHILDHOOD. It was recognized that children as a group were more exploited, deprived, and persecuted than Blacks, Indians, Chicanos, Women, Homosexuals, Foreigners, Jews, prison and mental hospital inmates, and the Poor. Perhaps overwhelmed by Guilt, Shame, and Anxiety in the face of these revelations, America rushed headlong into abolishing CHILDHOOD.

In the first year of the Great Children's Reform, all children of school age were taken from their homes and placed in luxurious Children's Parks—combined camps, playgrounds, and schools—in which all of American know-how and technology was mobilized for their happy growth and development. A search was made for the warmest, most loving and tender adults within the society, and these were put in charge of the children in numbers sufficient to free most of their time for play and affection.

Within a matter of months the Parks were filled with happy boys and girls who required very little discipline and who thrived on generous handouts of love. They played and they learned, learning and playing no longer being separable, and they grew up in happy accord among themselves and with their new adult friends.

And what happened to this new generation of "Park Children"?

[190]

They refused to join in Group Worship of the Group. They took no precautions against the Hebrew Disease.

They abandoned the pursuit of Pleasure Through Technology and sought simpler ways of life.

They showed hostility toward both the Democratic Owners of the People and the Republican Owners of Industry, and would not play Party Games. They laughed at the President, and some advocated a People's Party!

They refused to participate in such games as Rally 'Round the Missile, Recycling Our Enemies, and Throwing Candied Rocks. Instead they wanted to befriend the peoples of the Conquered Lands and inmates of the Zoo!

They refused to Make Up work for the Government; they eventually lost all interest in distinctions between the Elite and the Bureaucrats, between men and women, between children and adults.

And they all refused to suck.

Then while a nation of confused and anguished adults watched the destruction of NOW American values, these children embarked upon the worst abomination ever witnessed within a civilized society. They began to make love among themselves!

First adolescents, but then younger ones, finally even toddlers and infants began to take pleasure in each other's bodies. From the cradle to the bed, sensual and sexual whims were indulged without a trace of Guilt, Shame, or Anxiety. The body became nothing more nor less than an organ of lovemaking! The children even sucked—but only for pleasure and only among themselves, and *never* for the satisfaction of adults.

No one wanted to hurt these children. No one wanted to reinstate the Misery of CHILDHOOD. But American Civilization was at stake!

First the adults reinstated Ridicule Without Love, then Beatings and Blame, Deprivation, Loneliness and

[191]

Isolation, and so on. Each new technique worked for a while; then the children regained the upper hand and again took delight in each other. Meanwhile the older adolescents from the Parks joined in massive peaceful resistance under this banner:

> Mankind will know
> Love and peace
> When peoples of all ages
> Touch each other.

Reimposing CHILDHOOD upon the children took the combined forces of NAMS and its cadres of Officials, the financial resources of United American Goodwill Industries, Inc., and the troops of its major subsidiary, Investors Unlimited for Defense (IUD). Vast numbers of older children were killed, and America became a Conquered Land within itself, until CHILD-HOOD was reinstated in the Houses.

Once the government was again in control, it was easy to replicate and refine the Misery of Oldtime American Family Life within the Houses. The all-important *amnesia* was then found to manifest itself naturally as a defense against the Misery, and to this day Officials are only called upon in extreme cases to use their special technologies—drugs, conditioning, Pleasure Hospitalization, or Capping. No one *wants* to recall his early years for fear of reliving the Misery within himself. Thus each citizen is forever imprinted with the for-gotten lessons of CHILDHOOD, forever obedient to principles he cannot recall. Thus an unadulterated supply of Good Citizens is ensured for NOW and for All Time in America.

Parents, let Official History ease your task by proving the necessity of Misery. Do not suffer from Oldtime Guilt, Shame, and Anxiety over your treatment of your children. Instead, remember this—each Misery you inflict builds a Better Citizen for NOW America.

Enjoy Career Day! Enjoy the little Cocksuckers!

[192]

22nd Entry

"We will have to go into hiding or leave America soon," Gambol told me as we sat down to breakfast after the long night alone.

"First I have to visit the Houses," I said quickly.

"What Houses?"

"The ones where we were brought up."

"What are you talking about?"

"Gambol, I have begun to remember my CHILD-HOOD."

"No one—"

"My name was Timmy in the House of Ridicule Without Love."

Her face was chalky, her eyes a deeper brown within the chalk.

"My name was Jill in the House of Beatings and Blame," she said.

I sat down an arm's length away from her.

"Our parents beat us every day, Rogar. It was never me, it was never my friend across the hall or the one down the hall, but every night you could hear the

[193]

beatings, the slapping sounds, and the little cries. Then in the morning they would tell us we were all to blame. And we behaved and we begged forgiveness, but the Beatings and the Blame never let up. Every night as we tried to fall asleep we would hear the slaps and the little cries."

Tears rolled down her face.

"Then one night I couldn't stand it any more, and I found the door where the noises came from and I opened it. There was my mother slapping a little child, and every time the child would cry out, my father would look up from his Q-tube program and complain that they were disturbing him. And I begged them, 'Do it to me instead!' But they ignored me, Rogar. All three of them went on as if I wasn't there."

Gambol blinked to blot out the scene.

"I ran back to my room and huddled in my bed, listening to the slaps and cries."

She pulled up her knees to her chest and clung to herself.

"By morning, I was certain I was the only real person in the world. When I got out of bed, it was like stepping into a dream."

I moved closer to her and kissed her softly.

"They gave me tests and they tried me on pep-up pills, sedatives, tranquilizers. But they never gave up the Beatings and the Blame, and they never let me have a beating of my own. I became a person who watches, and soon I noticed a lot of the children were beating

[194]

themselves. Sometimes they would ask other children to beat them too, not directly but by being cruel or whiny. But I never beat myself, and I never let anyone else push me into beating them. And my parents and the other children lost interest in me, and no one ever touched me. Rogar, you are the first person to touch me."

She stretched out on the floor and I lay down beside her.

"It makes me marvel that you can love," I said.

"There was someone before you, a little boy named Kenny, and he lived in the House with me. I was five or six, and he was older, seven or eight. We made love."

"You touched each other?"

"We made love, Rogar."

"In the Bag? At age five?"

"There were no Bags in the Houses. We made love, and it was good."

She was matter-of-fact, as if this were her only normal memory.

"He would grin and laugh and make little screeches as his body moved above me. That's how they caught us. And no one ever saw him again."

She turned her head against my shoulder, and I held her with a sweetness that made my fingers tremble.

"I'm ready to tell you something important," she began again. "I feel pregnant, Rogar. I could feel it the day it happened."

"*Feel* it?"

"The first time we made love so beautifully—I felt a

little crackle and a swoop in my side. Yes, you made me
go crackle and swoop, and my egg came down to meet
your sperm."

It sounded mystical to me.

"I can feel my pregnancy in my breasts. They're
getting ready. There's a fullness in my womb, too. And I
want the baby. I'd like to name it after your friends
from the Twentieth Century, Soft Touch if it's a girl,
Sunspots if it's a boy. I've stolen an old medical book
from the library, and I'm sure we can deliver the baby
by ourselves. People have done it since time began. But
we'll have to hide or leave America, because from the
pictures in the book, I'll be as big as a Stack of Cubes."

I touched her breasts, her belly. "I like the names
you picked. What a mighty pregnant woman you'll
become."

But before I can think about a child—before I can
think about myself as a father—I will have to face what
was done to me in my own CHILDHOOD.

23rd Entry

The next morning Gambol Bubbled me to work, and that afternoon I went by the Official Bubble Pad and took off in one of their Bubbles. It was as easy as stealing an Oldtime car.

Within fifteen minutes I had crossed the city, flying higher than I'd ever flown, Passing Through the Eye on the Official level at Needletop. The stream of commuters obscured my presence, and the only Officials I saw were preoccupied with traffic surveillance.

Within minutes I reached the city's largest Restricted Area—the old site of the St. Elizabeth's Mental Hospital and Preventive Detention Center. I felt nearly certain it would turn out to be a House, perhaps my very own.

The shimmering Electronic Haze could strip off my negative charge, but I saw Official Bubbles pouring in both directions through a break within the Haze—commuter rush was on—and I glided undetected into the Restricted Area.

It was immense, with giant buildings interspersed with many Eggs, a small city hidden within the haze. A gas sign hung in the air toward the center of the area: HOUSES!

I dropped onto a Pad and took a conveyor that wrapped around an enormous round building with hundreds of side-by-side cavelike doorways perforating it in a single honeycomb layer. A sign read: Reformed HOUSE for Children and Old People.

Over one small honeycomb doorway was a makeshift hand-printed sign:

Welcome home, son!

Two people were standing inside, a woman and a man. The woman had a chain around her neck with a plaque over her breasts that read "Mom"; the man had a similar plaque reading "Dad."

"I'm T. E. P. Rogar," I sputtered.

"T. E. P. Rogar, O.B., O.B.P.," said Mom.

"You're my parents, and you remember me?"

"Of course, son," Dad said with a mixture of warmth and irritation that felt very familiar to me. "This is your home, too, hardly changed in the twenty-five years since we last saw you."

"But you recognize me?"

"How could Dad and I forget? We've waited so long for you to return."

"But nobody returns to CHILDHOOD."

[198]

"You have," Mom pointed out. "Why didn't you come back sooner? Would it have been so hard to take a little trip across town to see your poor old mother?"

"Mom, I don't understand. You must know that everyone in America is afraid to go home—"

"And they'll blame it on us poor old mothers."

"Besides, son, your Mom and I expected more from you."

I am trying to recapture what they looked like and how they treated me, when I realize: "You can't be my parents. You both can't be more than fifty years old."

"We're only trying to protect you," Dad says.

"What are you talking about?"

"We didn't want to tell you, but when you became so successful and still wouldn't visit your parents, your mother died of a broken heart."

"And after your father talked to your Autonomie," says Mom, "he was never the same again. But we're still glad to be your parents. You've done better than all your brothers and sisters."

Another figure materializing out of the background, an Official offering me a pill with great solicitation.

"I don't want medicine. I want to see the children!"

"What?" The Official perks up. "Are you some kind of pervert?"

"He's nothing like that, are you?" Mom starts crying, without tears.

"Please, son, think of your mother," Dad says.

"I came to see the children, not you two."

[199]

"Son!" cries Mom. "Not in front of the Official!"

"The children," I repeat.

"Listen, you, we have treatments for your kind."

"Let him see the children, if that's what he wants." Dad's tone is careful, almost threatening.

"You're sure? You'll take Official Responsibility for this?"

"But we should protect him." Mom is still crying very drily.

"I am going in to see the children, if they're here, if they exist."

"He's Mentally Ill," the Official says to no one in particular.

But my parents are leading the way into the House.

We walk through dark corridors gradually lightening, around one corner and then another, onto carpets and into soft indirect light with happy music piping from the walls. We pass a poster, "This is the first day of the rest of your life," and another, "War is not good for children and other living things," and still another, "Children come from love." There is a natural-color 3-D reproduction of a woman nursing an infant at her pink breast.

I pass one room marked Q-tube Study Hall, another marked Electronic Gymnasium, and another called ZOOM BOOM ROOM.

The ROOM!

That reflex dread again, but my parents are smiling as if they expect happy recognition.

[200]

"Which of the children would you like to see?" my father asks.

"My real brothers and sisters."

The Official snickers.

"Son, don't you remember anything about your own family? They're *all* your brothers and sisters."

A door labeled "Nursery" catches my eye and I pull it open.

It's a room full of blacks—large, full-breasted women, all of them nursing infants smaller than I've ever imagined: holding, rocking, and cooing over them.

All the babies are white.

I recall a faint image of a dark face leaning over me, and I feel a special warmth I've never experienced in my adult life.

Back in the corridor, Mom makes a terrible face. "They're the only ones who will do the work," she whispers.

"A long time ago, many of the infants wouldn't grow up," the Official explains. "They lost interest in things and died before we could condition them for NOW America. So now we use these women for the very little ones."

"And where do the babies come from?" I ask as casually as I can.

Everyone laughs at me.

"Is it a secret?"

"No, just that you wouldn't believe all the ways we can do it nowadays."

[201]

But my Hebrew genes slipped through!

Stopping at a door marked "Toddlers," I walk in upon two dozen little children playing amid electronic toys, flashing lights, bells, and happy music. All of them are naked and glistening; little cocks and cunts, baby asses, sweet grinning faces, all enjoying a carnival atmosphere.

The activity and the noise stop as I approach.

One little boy stares at me, grabs his cock and shrieks hysterically.

A little girl begins sobbing.

The children cower around Mom and Dad, crowing, sobbing, and pointing at me. Several are peeing or pulling at themselves frantically; one lets out an enormous bowel movement.

The Official pinches me out by the elbow and says, "Have you seen enough? Have you done enough?"

I break from his grasp and race down the hall past one door and then another, up an electronic stairway, around another corner; I pause in front of a ZOOM BOOM ROOM but then head for the end of the corridor where a familiar sign is blinking:

Exist—Exit—Exit—Exist

I burst in upon an enormous room with benches upon benches of old people packed together, all nodding in their sleep. Their heads are shaved and Capped, wires stretching aloft to great booms which slowly swing high above them as if in time to a waltz.

[202]

A sign is flashing red: *Sleep.* And the old heads are bobbing peacefully beneath their wires, skull Caps, and great booms. The light flashes *Awake!* And the faces perk up, heads still bobbing rhythmically beneath their wires.

I back out and walk slowly down the corridor to where Mom, Dad, and the Official are patiently awaiting me.

"I'm sorry you had to see that one," says the Official. "Most of the other Exit-Exist Rooms are much neater—transistorized and run by remote control."

"There, Timmy, you'll be all right," says Mom.

"Our son's name is Rogar, Mother," says Dad.

"T. E. P. Rogar," I repeat to bolster myself up. My legs are wobbly. "But how did I ever get a name like that, Mom?"

"Why, Timmy, you made it up yourself, you Silly Thing. We gave you children a lot of freedom."

"Now take your medicine," Dad says.

"Please, Timmy, for your poor old mother."

"It's either these pills or the medicine dart," the Official warns me.

And then the Cap or the Pleasure Probe.

"I still haven't seen the older children."

"More?" asks the Official. "You want to see more?"

"He always was stubborn," Dad says.

"Oh, let him have his way one more time. He always was my favorite." As she speaks, she glances at my Ball Pack.

[203]

I point past a ZOOM BOOM ROOM toward a door labeled Mature Cocksuckers. "That room."

They don't move to stop me, and I walk in.

I am confronted with five rows of boys and girls, Cocksuckers eight or nine years old, each busily at work over his Q Tube. They are fully dressed, in short skirts and tight pants, with stripes, dots, and a few gay patches. Snug blouses and shirts are fitted to their young figures, and some are wearing beads or a pendant around the neck. Nearly all, boys and girls alike, have long but neatly tailored hair.

The classroom walls are covered with student drawings, science project posters on Bubbling, and technical drawings about the Needle Eye. Pasted on the blackboard is a large yellow sunny face with a marvelous arc of a smile.

A young boy looks up from his Tube and notices me. He giggles and covers his mouth.

Laughter breaks out, and a few children stand up to point at me.

A single voice: "Where did he come from?"

"The ZOOM BOOM ROOM," somebody shrieks. "It's the new ZOOM BOOM ROOM MAN!"

Within an instant, every child is sitting still and silent, apparently absorbed at his Q Tube. I cannot tell that anything has happened except for one boy's hair out of place, a hitch in another's breathing, a trembling hand.

A little girl passes out at her Q Tube.

[204]

The Official comes in and carries her off.

Rushing out, I reach the corridor in time to see the girl being carried through the door of the ZOOM BOOM ROOM.

I throw my weight against the door but it does not budge.

The Official is behind me, looking very stern and disappointed.

"I wouldn't do that, Rogar. Besides, only Mom or Dad can send you there."

"Even if you won't think of your poor old mother," says Dad, "think of the other children. Some of them downstairs are still crying and wetting themselves."

My Mom takes the pill from the Official with a flourish as if she'd swallow it herself if she only could. Then she hands it to me.

I throw the pill down.

"Then go to your ROOM," Mom orders me, and it's as if I am being snatched away by some enormous hand upon my neck.

In an instant, I am there.

Where?

I look around and I don't see *anything!*

The child? Is she with me?

Do they make the children stay alone in here?

No, I'm the one who's alone.

In where?

A small bare room with translucent walls?

"Hello?"

My voice is sucked out of me and lost amid an enormous

```
                    ZOOM
        ZOOM                    BOOM
        TOMB        ZOOM        BOOM
    BOOM            ZOOM
                    ROOM                ROOM
        BOOM        WOMB        TOMB
        ZOOM        ZOOM    BOOM
```

My ears are ringing and vibrating with this sound like a million cymbals going off all around me—at a great distance and yet deep inside my head—through and through me.

And my body is beginning to feel weightless and unanchored, my hands seem miles away and unattached, my feet won't respond to my command and seem stretched out far away at the end of someone else's body.

I'm floating on my back, weightless in a bed without substance.

My bed . . .

How long will they do this to me?

"Let me out!"

But my voice is gone again amid the Zooming and the Booming, and I shrink in size, and I grow in size, and I have no size because I'm nowhere except in—

The room is growing dark.

I'll be all alone like this, all night in the dark!

[206]

I press my palms upon my head to keep it from expanding—to keep it from shrinking into a speck—and my head is empty except for all this sound, the lonely, empty, hollow, endless noise.

I am disappearing into

EMPTY SPACE

I am becoming

NOTHING

"Mom? Dad? Anybody?"
The Zooming and the Booming let up.
The light begins to return.
My body gathers in a little closer to myself.
I hear my own small voice from CHILDHOOD: I remember that everything will be all right if I apologize, beg forgiveness, and promise to behave.
Instead I roar:

I CAN DO WITHOUT YOU NOW!
I AM A MAN!

With these words, I find myself back in the corridor.
"What do you think you're doing out of your room?" the Official demands.
I am facing him set to defend myself from his medicine dart.
Mom looks shocked. "You disobeyed us?"

[207]

"I'm surprised at you, son," Dad says.

"Don't either of you ever call me 'son' again."

"That's how he got out of his room," Mom wails.

"Who do you think you are?" Dad demands.

"I'll tell you!" I reply too loudly, and all three freeze expectantly, shoulder-to-shoulder in an absurd tableau.

"If these aren't your parents," the Official asks very slowly, "then what are you doing here?"

"WHO AM has sent me."

"You are Mentally Ill!" The Official poises to throw the medicine dart at me, and I set myself to dodge it.

"If you miss, you'll be unarmed," I warn him.

"You're dangerous, that's what you are." He turns to Mom and Dad. "He's got to learn his lesson. We'll make *him* be the one to send the children to their rooms."

Tears stream down my face.

"Tears!" The Official points at me with the dart. "A Jew! A Hebrew Agent-Priest SPREADING TEARS." He begins stalking around me in a wide circle, like a dog sniffing out a weakness.

I hear Mom moaning, "Our son the Jew!" and then Dad's simple utterance from the past, "Stop crying this minute, Timmy."

It paralyzes me for an instant, and the Official lunges at me with the dart. I grab his arm with both my hands, avoid his thrust, and fling him like a sack against the wall.

[208]

As he comes bouncing back, I grab his hand, dart and all, and plunge the needle into his chest.

The Official goes into a convulsion, his arms and legs flailing about, his belly pitching up and down. It looks for all the world as if he is being fucked to death by an insect bobbing up and down upon his chest.

Soon he is dead.

When I turn around, Mom is staring at his body, her lips parted.

Dad turns and runs down the hall, shouting, "Murderer! Stop the Murderer!"

I catch him from behind in two strides and grab him by the neck chain of his "Dad" plaque. The sign snaps back and cuts him down like a karate chop to the throat. He lies dead upon the floor, a stuffed puppet who has lost his strings.

"You're a Dead Dad," I say with no remorse.

Mom is lying on the floor, her legs spread wide, her bottom exposed. "It's you I want, son, you. You're the real man of the House. You always were my favorite!"

Mom will do anything to stop me from going free. It has always been that simple and it always will be. There is nothing more to be said about the whole business of motherfucking.

She is still groveling upon her back, her old thighs gyrating, her "Mom" plaque hiked up around her neck like a wooden collar. I could cut off her breath with it and be done with her. Then I might escape without my identity becoming known.

[209]

A siren is wailing. I hear the sounds of many running feet.

"Just once, Timmy, just once like you always wanted."

But now she's scrambling away from me, still on her back, like an overturned crab. "You can't, Timmy, you can't kill your poor old mother!"

24th Entry

Amid sirens, flashing lights, the sounds of running feet and shouts, I made my escape without seeing a single person.

It was too easy taking off in my Bubble; too easy floating along gaily amid outbound Bubbles winking in the sunlight. Do they want me to escape? So they can track me down to my Journal and to Gambol?

They may be at Gambol's already.

Gambol, being dragged away . . .

I brought my Bubble down fast upon Gambol's Stack of Cubes and raced for the entrance to the Chute. Halfway through the door, I noticed a wisp of color at the handle—the slender pink ribbon she had once tied around my Bubble's foot.

This was no day for tricks.

I turned over the *Welcome Groupers* mat and found a note:

> Hurry away from here!
> Meet me where we first touched.

Gliding in toward the mountain Pad, I saw another Bubble parked there—an Official Bubble! I veered away, nearly tumbling out of control but nonetheless catching a glimpse of the tall figure of J. A. R. D. Gambol standing high upon our rock.

In a few seconds I settled down beside her stolen Bubble.

Our hug between the Bubbles left me satisfied and alive.

"You escaped from your mother," Gambol said as if she knew everything.

"Yes, but I should have killed her. She must have reported me and sent them after you."

"Rogar, your mother didn't have to report you. When I got home after work, before you had time to reach the House, an Official was already waiting in my Cube. He told me you would fuck your mother and be caught in the act, and that would end your political career."

I let out a low whistle.

"That's how I knew you'd escape. I was certain nothing could make you want your mother after having me."

I grinned. "But how did you escape?"

"Rogar, the Official said he had to take me away to Cap me, but first, since he was such a great Dynamo, he'd give me one last fucking in the Bag. I thought of you telling me how I'm too much for any NOW American, and so while he was pumping his cock into the Bag, I slipped the Bag away and took him into my body."

Her great soft palm and tapered fingers touched mine.

"He screamed and struggled, but I held him strongly. Then I let him go, and he hurled himself off the balcony of my Cube. He landed on the ledge ten stories down and lay there like a man sleeping."

We held hands, watching a single rocket streaming slowly toward the Conquered Lands.

Then Gambol pushed open her stolen Official Bubble and showed me what she had gathered: a medical book, tools, food concentrates, her painting clothes and materials, a portable microfilm writer for my work, and a thousand Capsule copies of my Journal, which she had made minutes before at NAMS. She had even brought along the tattered remnants of the Declaration of Independence.

As I climbed in beside her in the Bubble, I knew we had very little chance to survive the day—yet I felt happy; alive with love for myself and for Gambol, and free within myself and with this woman to make the best of whatever we could seize from life. We were smiling at each other, and so in touch we did not have to talk.

"We need a rocket ship," I said finally.

She laughed. "Let's steal one."

"In the Twentieth Century, Gambol, when anybody wanted to escape America, they got on board a plane, threatened the pilot and passengers, and demanded to be taken wherever they wanted to go."

"No. . . ."

"It worked many times, despite special guards and precautions. It could work for us, if we can find a weapon. Gambol, there *is* a weapon! A powerful weapon, ready for the picking."

"The Israeli MICROBOMB," she said. "The one sitting in the middle of the Ballroom at the White House!"

"You remember!" I was pleased with my only reader.

"But Rogar, your last information is nearly a century old."

"The White House is still boarded up. And besides, if the Bomb is no longer sitting there, then Israel may be gone as well."

Gambol climbed up into the pilot's side of the Bubble and handed me the box of Journal Capsules she had made for me.

"It's risky to take the time to scatter them," I said.

"It's your life's work, Rogar. Besides, those smug Officials are probably waiting for us to turn ourselves in at the Zoo."

She topcharged the Bubble, and we lifted off the Pad.

In a few minutes, we were over the outskirts of the People's Highrises, but I had no grandiose hopes for my impact upon America as I began to scatter the Capsules.

"Gambol, I feel that I've already had more than

most men in my lifetime. I've had you and I've had my work."

"I haven't had enough of you or my painting," she said. "And now we're starting a family."

A family of our own, to raise with all the love of life that we share!

I cast a few Capsules over the homes of the Republican Industrial elite and the Democratic Government elite, but I saved my largest handfuls for the Stacks of Cubes in the inner city where my colleagues, the Bureaucrats, live. Finally we sped over NAMS and did a pirouette over each giant monument, dropping these Seeds of the One.

In one swoop Gambol nearly impaled us on America's Most Proud Erection!

"The Zoo," Gambol said. "Let's not forget the Blacks."

We took a few turns over the nearest edge of the great black compound, but none of the Magnetic Fields crossed close enough to let us float our seeds down to them. Instead, I contented myself with dropping a large handful over an area where whites were fond of throwing Candied Rocks.

I changed seats with Gambol and turned the Bubble toward the boarded-up White House, while she went rummaging around in her supplies. She brought out a portable electric knife and flipped the switch: the blade vibrated and burned hot enough to sear meat, roasting each slice as it cut.

"I could hold off a man with this," she said.

I winced.

She pulled out her painting clothes, squirmed into them, and handed me a pair. "We can fight better in these."

"What an Israeli!" I said, using the Oldtime expression for military prowess.

"The clothes will also make it easier to break through underbrush around the White House."

I looked with admiration at this giant of a woman dressed in weird and awful-smelling clothes, with a hatchet and a flasher in her lap and a searing knife in her hand. And I was sure we would attract attention, but not a Bubble was within half a mile of ours.

"I feel safer in clothes," Gambol said. "More private, more like a person. And think what a time we'll have when we strip off each other's clothes!"

"It's going to give us a big advantage when we storm the rocket."

Only three minutes or less to the White House, but potentially a continent of GOUP between us and the rocket.

"Gambol, reach into my pants and pull off my Ball Pack and throw it out."

Gently she unloosened and unplugged me and removed the Ball Pack. Pushthrough Plastic engulfed her arm and then her hand came back empty.

She had already left her hardware behind.

So much for NOW American Technology.

In a minute we'd be above the White House, facing the problem of how to land.

[216]

"Rogar? If the MICROBOMB goes off, we're going to kill millions of people, aren't we? We're risking millions of people for our own freedom."

"Oh, no!" I cried out.

"What's the matter?"

"Down there. Look!"

The White House was in a cage—the entire area, from fence to fence, covered with a heavy wire mesh. Trees and tall tropical shrubs were growing up through it. We'd never before been close enough to notice the wire.

"At least we've got something springy to land on. Hang on!" I howled like a kid on his first Passage Through the EYE as I discharged the Bubble.

I saw us glancing off the cage and careening into a Stack of Cubes.

I saw us shattered on the cage, and impaled upon a dozen torn wire ends.

I saw us—*sitting in a giant magnolia tree!* We had punched right through the decayed wire mesh and landed as lightly as a balloon within the great branches.

A glance upward, and we knew we were going to have a hard time getting out through the hole again.

Alarms might be going off, and the White House was buried within a jungle.

I took the flasher and the hatchet, then turned and kissed my love long and tenderly. When I finally drew back, we both grinned at the bulge in my lap. It felt odd, a hard on in pants.

I pressed Gambol's belly, where our child was

[217]

growing, then left without a word and began crashing through the shrubs and weeds.

After pulling a few boards off a set of glass doors, I chopped away the handle and stepped into the White House.

My flasher disclosed a great room completely furnished, everything apparently untouched, including Oldtime carpets, pictures on the walls, and Oldtime vases and silver on the tables. A piano, too.

I passed signs of precipitous departure—trays and glasses and dishes, some broken and scattered about; several pairs of high-heeled shoes, a fur piece, a glass slipper.

I reached the Ballroom and saw it there—in the middle of the floor—a football-shaped object, black, and spiked like a huge sea anemone.

I would like to say that I stood paralyzed for an instant before I picked up the Microbomb, that I agonized before I laid a hand on it, that momentous thoughts popped in my brain as I touched it—but in fact I simply picked it up.

It was *very* heavy.

The spikes were not sharp, but they made it hard to handle by myself. While I held one spike in each fist, others dug into my knuckles and wrists. And the spikes were oddly shaped, for a function that eluded me.

And there was a red object sticking up—the Big Red Button. Had the Israeli Ambassador forgotten to press it? Or had Israel long ago discontinued the remote-control activation system? Had its mechanism corroded over the decades?

It could explode if I dropped it or jostled it in the Bubble.

A delayed fuse might be set to go off automatically in a few minutes.

Staggering through the mini-jungle with the lead porcupine in my arms, I came upon a remarkable sight: Gambol, standing in the midst of a monstrous magnolia tree heavy with blossoms, her back braced against the trunk, her arms pushing against the Bubble.

She heaved her weight against the Bubble, and it spilled from the tree, rolled several yards through the brush, and came to rest upright directly beneath the gaping hole in the wire cage.

In moments we were Bubbling along toward the Rocket Pad, with the Bomb in Gambol's lap.

Out of nowhere, an Official Bubble came bearing down upon us. He circled overhead with his rockets and we waved toward him gaily. He turned abruptly and took off in another direction.

Only then did we notice the big leathery green leaves and waxy white blossoms of a magnolia branch above us, its strong stem wrapped around the Bubble and caught in the Pushthrough Plastic portal. We sailed along toward the Rocket Pad like a triumphant Prince and Princess floating beneath a tropical canopy.

25th Entry

Ten huge rocket ships stood at attention on the Rocket Pad, one with a boarding escalator mounted beside it. A People Eater Bus was already crawling from the terminal to the rocket ship; a transparent caterpillar engorged with human beings.

"Rogar, there's no Bubble path across the field."

"Let me try the auxiliary rockets. We've got to land nearly on top of the rocket to gain surprise."

"Surprise?" Gambol laughed at the magnolia tree waving above us. "But let it wave!"

I fired the forward-thrust rockets and we jolted away; then I ignited the retrogrades, braking us in mid-air for an instant of motionless suspension. Down we went, forward thrusters and landing rockets going at once—thud—rolling over on the ground. While we dangled upside down from our straps for everyone to see, the Bubble rocked slowly to a standstill with the loose Microbomb clumping about on its spikes like a bloated drunken spider in the overturned top.

We scrambled out amid a crowd of naked gaping

Groupers and Officials, Gambol swishing about with her buzzing, burning knife. The crowd parted like a flock of park pigeons.

We raced to the boarding escalator and started up the spiral of moving stairs, a stewardess fleeing ahead of us.

Red lights flashed, the escalator came to a halt, and we burst through one of the portals of the ship just as it began to close. Inside, we raced up the corkscrew stairs through the seats and came crashing in behind the stewardess as she reached Pilot in the cockpit.

As Pilot stuck out his hand toward Gambol, she made a swipe at him with her blade. He staggered back against his instrument panel, his eyes bugging out at us—two maniacs dressed in baggy painted clothes, one carrying something like an iron porcupine, the other wielding a hot, sharp knife.

"This is a Microbomb," I told him.

"I don't care if it's the President's pet pig, you can't come in here."

"We'll all die if I press this Big Red Button. This is a hijacking."

"A what?"

"Fly us to Israel," Gambol said, "or we'll cut you both up and turn America into GOUP."

She made a swipe at the stricken stewardess and then punctuated it with a wink. That did it: Pilot turned pale.

"Tell your stewardess to clear out," I said, "and make sure no one else is on board. Then lock the hatches."

[222]

Gambol used her knife to prod the stewardess out ahead of her.

I ordered Pilot to sit down at his seat and stationed myself behind him, my finger on the Big Red Button, my right hand holding the hatchet above his head.

"You are going to take us to Israel."

"Midwestern towns don't *have* rocket pads."

"It's not in America. It's in the Conquered Lands."

He sprang bolt upright, banged his head on the flat side of my hatchet, and slammed back into his seat as if I'd clubbed him.

"Put on your safety belt and don't try to loosen it," I said.

He obeyed.

"All clear!" Gambol shouted from below.

Pilot closed the hatch.

By the time Gambol returned, the ship's radio was crackling: "Control Tower to Pilot ZAX! Control Tower to Pilot ZAX! What's going on up there?"

"Tell them to clear the Pad for takeoff," I said.

"They won't let me!"

"Tell them I'll turn America into GOUP if you don't take off."

Then the radio: "What's he talking about?"

"GOUP!" I shouted. "G-O-U-P! God's Original Universal Power!"

"He's got a hatchet, and His Girl's got an electric knife!" Pilot called out.

"I am not 'His Girl'!"

"What's this Bomb stuff?" the radio demanded.

I leaned into the radio and said as calmly as I could,

[223]

"You are endangering yourselves and several hundred million Americans. Call NAMS and ask for the Attorney General. Tell him we have the White House Microbomb and we're going to press the Big Red Button if Pilot doesn't take us where we want to go."

The radio: "And where is *that?*"

"Israel!"

The radio: "Will the people on board identify themselves while we call NAMS."

"T. E. P. Rogar, O.B., O.B.P., NAMS." And then to make sure it wouldn't sound like an Attitude Check, "The last Hebrew from America, bound for Israel."

"And J. A. R. D. Gambol, a Human Being with child!" she added joyfully.

Silence.

Until the radio burst out: "ZAX! Pilot ZAX! Don't panic! Don't panic!"

"Why not? Why not?" shouted Pilot.

I tapped him lightly with the hatchet.

The radio was giving off Control Room noises—talking, banging, occasional shouts, whines, and bleeps from communications equipment.

"They must have found out who we are," Gambol observed.

"Pilot!" the radio squawked. "Stay away from his Tears!"

"Oh, no," Pilot groaned.

More Control Room sounds:

That Dynamo is suspected of Jewish activities. Of Spreading Tears! Bulletin! Bulletin! That Good Lay pushed an Official to his death! Warning! Warning! That Dynamo is wanted for frackle-snazzle—peep! peep! peep!

Pilot fumbled frantically with the dials.

"I'll tell you what I'm wanted for," I informed Pilot. "I killed my father and rejected my mother."

The radio: "Await orders! Await orders! Do not take off!"

I leaned over Pilot and whispered into his ear: "If you don't take off instantly, I'll cry all over you."

He pulled several switches and pressed a button and the rocket rumbled. He pushed another set of buttons, leaned forward on a lever, and we lifted off the ground.

In seconds we were roaring through low clouds, and in seconds more the earth was receding like a distant dark slope.

I clutched the Microbomb with one hand and Pilot's chair with the other; Gambol braced herself against the wall.

The rocket tilted and then straightened out, and we began burning our way toward Israel.

I warned Pilot that if he failed to find Israel we'd all be going down among the Conquered Peoples. He nodded understanding. Rocket ships are instrumental in Recycling Our Enemies, and no rocket pilot would dare fall into enemy hands.

Pilot was now completely docile, and Gambol and I were able to exchange smiles and a quick kiss.

Below us lay a mass of gray that must be the ocean, but the gray was already darkening ahead of us.

[225]

"Land?"

"Must be North Africa," said Pilot.

"Follow the northern coast along the Mediterranean."

"Too late!" he exclaimed. "Up there, to the left, ten o'clock!"

Three small objects were speeding toward us.

"Manned Interceptors?"

"Too small. Attack rockets," he said dismally.

"Israeli?"

"They've got to be our own. We won the Good War and we have No More Enemies."

We braced for impact, but the three tiny rockets swooped over us like red birds coming to roost and then arranged themselves in formation a hundred yards ahead of us.

The radio: "This is the United Arab People's Defense Command. This is the United Arab People's Defense Command. Identify yourself! Identify yourself!"

"Oh, no, the Arabs!" I nearly dropped the Bomb. But Gambol did not flinch, and I regained my composure.

"Repeating for the last time: This is the United Arab People's Defense Command. You are surrounded by Arab Interceptors. You will be destroyed in ten seconds if you do not identify yourselves. Beginning the ten-second countdown:

"Ten.

"Nine.

"Eight.

"Seven.

"Six.

"Five.

"Four.

"Three—"

"This is T. E. P. Rogar," I blurted out. "O.B., O.B.P., NAMS, Chief Historian for Oldtime Twentieth Century. We're escaping from America. I am seeking political asylum in Israel!"

"Oh, why did I say *that?* Telling Truth to an Arab!"

The red rockets waggled their tails ahead of us.

The radio again: "Are you requesting permission to proceed under escort to Israel?"

"Yes! Yes!"

Israel exists!

"Are you carrying any armaments?"

"This is a passenger rocket," shouted Pilot. "And I'm not Jewish. I don't even *look* Jewish!"

Silence from the radio. Then: "Repeat, are you carrying armaments or weapons of any kind?"

"No!" Pilot howled.

"Begin a northern course away from the United Arab Defense Perimeter."

"They've detected our Bomb, and they're moving us away to blow us up," I told Gambol.

I filled my chest with air and bellowed: "I am a Hebrew, armed with an Israeli Microbomb. I will detonate the Bomb if you try to harm us."

"We repeat for the last time: Begin a northern

[227]

course in formation behind the lead Arab Interceptors."

"Stay on course toward Israel," I instructed Pilot.

Gambol buzzed her vibrator knife at him.

"Countdown," Arab Radio crackled. "Ten, nine, eight—"

"I'll turn you all to GOUP!" I yelled. "G–O–U–P–. God's Original Universal Power!"

The countdown stopped.

"Don't get hysterical. We are trying to connect you directly with Israel. Don't get hysterical."

"Israel." I grinned at Gambol. "Israel!"

"Stand by. Stand by. We are switching you directly to the Israeli Defense Command. Do not take evasive action. Do not take threatening action."

Another squadron of red rockets swarmed around us, but I was no longer afraid.

I found myself thinking of the people whose lives I had placed second to my own freedom when I seized the Bomb, those millions of Americans struggling in such futility to overcome Guilt, Shame, and Anxiety. I was going into exile feeling a deep sadness inseparable from my escape. Israel *and* America would be my two nations.

Gambol came over to me and put her head upon my shoulder. This woman who had killed a man with her passion and who had so brazenly commandeered the rocket ship let out a great silent wail against my ear. Here, high above the earth, the center of all feeling seemed held within my arms.

And now that our escape seemed near to completion, I tried to include Pilot. "You may not think you look Jewish, but everyone in the Western World has at least a trace of Jewish blood within his veins, and everyone who can think has more than a trace of Jewish Thought in his mind. It's a matter of accepting *yourself.*"

But would Israel accept him?

And Gambol and me?

Israel had suspended the Law of Return more than a century ago to stop the ransoming of Jews. Was the Law again in effect?

And had Israel revived the Law of Return to save American Jewry? The Good War was over at the time, and Israel had the Bomb with which to threaten America—if the Israelis had been willing to risk themselves for other Jews. It didn't fit together, the extinction of Jewish Life in America and the survival of Israel.

I was pondering this unknown history when the radio crackled again: "This is the Israeli Defense Command. Identify yourself."

Tears rolled down my face, and Pilot struggled in his straps in panic. I touched him on the shoulder. "It's a myth," I said gently. "Jewish Tears never hurt anyone." Then, loudly and solemnly, to the radio: "My name is T. E. P. Rogar. I am an American Hebrew in flight to Israel, seeking political asylum and freedom. I have with me J. A. R. D. Gambol, an American woman, and the pilot we've forced to fly us here."

"Do you really have the White House Microbomb on board?"

"Yes."

"I'll be damned! Abba did forget to press the Big Red Button!"

I heard laughter, and a man saying something I couldn't understand.

"I don't speak Hebrew. No one in America knows any Hebrew."

"Yes, we're aware of your cultural situation . . . In a few moments the red Arab interceptors will be joined by blue and white Israeli interceptors. You will follow them and land according to instructions."

"Just one question, please. I don't understand the Arab interceptors. Aren't the Arabs under Israeli occupation?"

"What good is a Jew with an Arab on his back? We didn't conquer them, we liberated them."

The sky grew full with red, white, and blue interceptors. It could have been a July Fourth celebration.

We were given landing instructions, and as our rocket turned its nose up and began the slow backward descent I could see a marvelous city. In the center were buildings older than anything in America, but ringing them were great spirals and arches, and an enormous six-pointed star gleaming in the distance, set within a silver ring—a monument that dwarfed America's Most Proud Erection.

A great banner—"SHALOM!" it read—was waving on a high lookout deck crowded with spectators.

We settled in an easy landing, and Pilot waited in the cockpit, as we had been instructed. I picked up the

[230]

Bomb and stepped out into an elevator tower. Far below, a great crowd awaited us.

As we descended we could see that most people were dressed, though rather scantily. Here and there I spotted colored hats, plumes, and other decorations.

Perhaps fifty feet off the ground, Gambol nudged me. "They look more like me than like O.B.P.'s," she said.

Sure enough, the closer we got, the more plump and full-breasted the women appeared; and still closer up, their faces looked different from NOW Americans—their features more prominent, their smiles more open.

Gambol's face broke open with joy as she pointed toward a woman with a tiny baby in her arms. Yes, there were little children, sitting on grownups' shoulders and playing with each other.

We stepped onto the ground, my arms aching with the weight of the Bomb, and a very old and chubby lady began to plod forward to meet us in front of the rocket. She was wearing a plain loincloth with one shoulder strap; by her side, a young man was carrying a microphone.

"She looks ancient," I whispered.

"Centuries old," Gambol whispered back.

The old lady was standing in front of us now, and as the young man held up the microphone, the crowd grew silent.

"In the name of the Chosen People, I welcome you to Israel!" the old lady proclaimed. "You are among the first American Jews to reach Israel in 112 years."

"I am not a Jew," Gambol replied, and a great silence fell over the crowd.

A single voice shouted, "Gentile!"

The old woman looked long and hard at me, and I answered, "I *am* a Jew. My Visions are my evidence. My Visions have become reality."

The man with the microphone gasped. "Visions are your only proof?"

There were catcalls from one section of the crowd where I thought I saw a small band of aged bearded men trying to throw stones at us.

I placed the Bomb upon the ground in a gesture of peace. When I arose, Gambol was reaching for my hand, and we stood together looking out upon a vast throng of silent strangers.

"Who are you two?" the old woman demanded.

I began to say, "We are who we are," but it no longer seemed enough.

I turned to Gambol; she, too, was unready to answer.

Instead we paused to look around more carefully.

In front of us stood a long row of several dozen turnstiles, each with a Party Sign above it and a long queue of party members waiting to greet us:

The Zionist Party: Kiss the Ground and You Can Enter.
The Religious Party: Cover Your Head and Pray
     Your Way Through.
The Liberal Party: Adopt an Arab on Your Way In.
The Communist Party: Leave Everything at the
     Turnstile.
The Capitalist Party: Welcome Tourists.

[232]

"That's Customs," the old lady said. "You have to Declare Yourself with us."

"I don't like it," I said.

"I refuse!" Gambol told her.

"Then you two can join the Coalition *I* lead. We'll adapt to anyone."

I shook my head and so did Gambol.

"But what other choice do you have?" the old lady asked.

Gambol and I looked at each other and then we turned our backs on the Parties, the old lady and her escort, and we stared out to sea.

"We might have a chance to make a life for ourselves here," I told Gambol. "But it doesn't feel right to me."

"They already want me to become something other than I am," she said.

Then we heard the shouting.

"Look over there!" I pointed toward a far corner of the field where a small band of demonstrators was waving at us from behind a line of security police. One demonstrator was holding up a black shrouded sign, "European Jewry," crossed out with a Swastika, and another was holding up a similar mourning sign, "Russian Jewry," crossed out with a Hammer and Sickle. And then they gave a mighty shout as they unfurled an enormous banner:

SAVE AMERICAN JEWRY
Save *All* the Individuals of America

"Yes!" we shouted back, and the demonstrators

broke through the restraining line and came running toward us, the freedom banner streaming overhead, the police in pursuit.

The old lady and her young man were jabbering at us:

"They're not even an Official Party."

"They tried to smuggle arms into America."

"They wanted to invade Long Island with a guerrilla force."

"They'll do *anything* to save a few Individuals!"

Gambol and I picked up the Bomb; I gestured toward the Big Red Button, and the police stopped dead in their tracks.

In moments we were rallying around the freedom banner—hugging, kissing, shaking hands, and introducing ourselves. There were half-a-dozen Americans in the group—three couples who had escaped ahead of us—and we could see from the determination in their faces that we shared the same mission. We were ready to return to America.

The old lady was mumbling something about how much we had to lose and how easy it would be for us to stay in Israel; and a phalanx of police was charging across the field toward us.

Half a dozen hands picked up the Bomb while a dozen more bodies shielded us, and again the police went into a quick retreat.

Someone took the microphone and announced, "We Israelis will stay here to do what we must do."

Individuals from nearly every Party came running out to join his group in a circle around us.

[234]

"You'll risk us all—Israel itself—for *them?*" the old woman demanded.

The Israeli said something to her in Hebrew and then turned to us and translated: "Israel may yet become a light to the nations."

The Bomb was light in our many hands as we carried it back on board the rocket ship.